CHARMED BY 3

AN AGE GAP CONTEMPORARY REVERSE HAREM

BARBI COX

VALERIE

*C*losing my eyes, I let myself remember those three sexy men. Hunter with his tousled light brown curly hair, tan skin, wild and cocky attitude but with a body that begs to be licked and touched. Chase, he's so smart and oh, so easy on the eyes. He had that almost bad boy rocker look with the sides of his head shaved, that single tattoo spreading across his chest, big arms straining against his shirt, and even those glasses. They made him look more dangerously sexy as if that's even possible. It almost feels illegal looking at him. All of them!

Then Lief.

Lief the enigma. His honey-brown hair, pale blue eyes, hint of a beard, and those hot Norse tattoos that tracked up his whole right arm and maybe further. Beyond all that, he was huge, at least six foot three or four, and broad. Ugh, I'd felt exactly how proportional his *everything* was when we'd danced together. Who am I kidding? All of them were hung.

Hunter was a bit of an arrogant asshole from the first time I met him all the way through to the wedding, but the naughty, delicious things he'd said in my ear while grinding against me had made me wet on the spot. Even though I hate it, I've always been a sucker for a bad boy and Hunter is that times ten.

Chase knew just how to touch me, got hard from my dance moves alone, and his determination to please and tempt didn't go to waste. He read me just right, made me feel hot and valuable, then gave me an incredible night that has fueled plenty of good solo sessions for me.

But Leif. Oh, Leif. There's something so dark and cold about him which means he has sexy secrets I'd kill for. The gentle offer for more than a dance in my ear and the most mediocre compliment ever had set my skin on fire. But when I'd been ready to capitalize, he'd been on the phone, then he walked away.

So I'd turned my attention back on Chase and had absolutely no regrets. Honestly, it had been the hottest night of my life. He did more than satisfy me. He loved my rough side, took every bite, and gave them right back to me. He manhandled me, gave me control just to take it back. Our back and forth was insane. He was intense, we were loud, and it was pure ecstasy. The kind of sex and passion a girl dreams about. And we'd just kept going and going. Round after round until we passed out and nearly woke up around lunchtime.

But I haven't heard a word from him since.

At least my vibrator is reliable. Plus, there's no confusion, shitty personality, risk, or compromise. It's just all about me and I get myself off every time ... alone. Then roll over and go to bed ... alone. Which used to be fine, but now that I'm staying in on another Friday night looking at a weekend with nothing to do but study, I hate my lack of relationship.

I have friends and colleagues, but ... but seeing Sophie so happy with four men wrapped around her finger has me questioning if getting my Ph.D. is the end-all be all that I want.

Maybe it's time to start considering a regular partner instead of my vibrator for emergencies. I could handle an actual boyfriend, or at least a regular friends' with benefits. At least I'd spend less on batteries that way.

Scrolling through my phone, I find Chase's number but I hesitate. It's been weeks. Do I want him to capitalize on a booty call? Won't I look desperate? And what would he think of me after? Would he want more than I'm ready to give or go and brag to his brother?

"Crap!" I toss my phone. "Can I just turn this brain off for one weekend so I can get laid?"

Since that's not going to happen and thinking of these three sexy men is just making lust pool in my belly. I eat my pizza and try to focus on a documentary a professor recommended. When that doesn't cloud out fantasies of all three men playing a tug of war over me in bed, I check my emails and see a forwarded invitation from Sophie for some charity event. Gunner is going to represent their company and it's just an hour away. Tomorrow.

A reason to get out of the house – check. A reason to get dressed up and sexy – check.

A chance to get laid and stop thinking about that trio of tall handsome hunks that offered me themselves– double-check. Maybe Gunner will be a good wingman and do the job well. I email back saying I'll go and print the invite before changing for bed and getting a solid twelve-hour hibernation in.

The next day, I get some good quality studying done, so I feel productive for school, then get ready for the event. I style my auburn hair into lanky curls and pull on a black glittery cocktail dress that's backless and says, "down to fuck." After getting stiletto heels on, putting pepper spray in my purse, and applying my wine-red lipstick,

I pull on a sweeping white coat to keep myself warm through D.C.'s lingering winter.

I check myself one more time in the mirror, then walk down to my car and I fight my way through traffic with the help of my GPS.

I can't believe the venue. It's huge, classy in that modern art way, and somehow makes me feel like I'm underdressed despite wearing the best thing in my closet. There are also so many people. Most of the guys are dressed the same, so I have no clue how I'm going to find Gunner by wandering.

Taking a slow breath, I reach into my little purse for my phone. I'm sure I still have his number saved.

"Val!" I hear a second later.

Gunner crushes me against him, nearly breaking my back. I push against his chest while laughing. "Thanks for the back crack, but don't break me!"

"I just don't know my own strength." He flexes his arms.

He's trying to hide it, but I can see the bags under his eyes and the exhaustion in his eyes. He's trying too hard. I tap his nose. "You look tired, Gunner. Pregnancy not as much fun as you hoped?"

I let him vent about it as he guides me to a table, then he sighs. His venting is different from Sophie's at least. He shrugs, then pauses. "I love Sophie so much. The mood swings are a little hard, but I want to do everything for her, want to be all over and when she's not jumping us, she's trying to get a million things done."

I believe it. There's a whole nursery to put together, a ton of things to have ready for when the baby comes home, and life doesn't stop to give even a second for Sophie to relax.

Gunner continues. "Nick knows just what to do. Just what to get, all of it. Holden gets to cuddle her all day, and Roman keeps her fed, so

4

I'm trying to help out with something other than sex and it's a lot." He chuckles.

"I'm sure you have plenty to offer and I *know* how much she loves you, Gun. There's just a lot going on with her hormones. She's growing a whole human." I remind him.

"Yeah, I know. That's why I'm telling you and not her. I'm over-thinking and you're my sounding board. Congrats."

"Does that mean I'm your bestie too now?" I tease, bumping his hip.

"Something like that." He chuckles.

I glance at a group of guys as they walk in. Some are promising, that's for sure. I lean over to whisper in Gunner's ear as if anyone is paying attention to us. "Do you still have those wingman skills you bragged about forever ago?"

"Oh, you want to find out?" He rubs his hands together. "Point me at a man and watch me work for you, Val."

I look around, trying to see if any guy immediately catches my eye. Instead, I get caught up in the event itself. It's some kind of silent auction which means rich people are tying their pride to their wallets and happily one-upping each other. I bet none of them bid at the exact price of the things. They go over, just to show they can.

I'd love a class specifically on studying the psychology of different classes of people. The way it can cause social dilemmas and funda-mentally alter experiences and sense of self. People watching is the best form of casual study. The way people interact, where they place importance, and the way they hold themselves, says so much about where they are mentally. It's so entertaining to me.

Like Gunner, looking around while sipping from his drink, craning his neck, then smiling at me when I catch him and pausing to down his whole glass. If I didn't know better I would say he's waiting for someone else and doesn't want me to know.

"Who else has been invited?"

"Half of the upper class in D.C." He shrugs.

"Don't avoid the question."

"Would you rather I finally strip for you? Is that what tonight is about? Trying to see me shirtless after all this time because you couldn't at the strip club?" He smirks.

I drum my fingers on the table. The quieter I am, the more he'll spill. As predicted, he fills the silence. "It's not like I know every millionaire, just a lot of them. And you cross paths enough times and you start to see familiar faces, you might even see some tonight."

"You're being extra cagy tonight." I point out. "Can't you just tell me what I'm in for? It won't kill you."

"You *hope* it won't kill me." He teases. "But you'd feel really bad if it did."

Trying the silent stare again, he just narrows his eyes and focuses on me like we're having a staring contest. I shake my head. "Just tell me. I'm not a fan of suspense."

"Consider it a surprise."

I take a drink from my glass and rub the back of my neck. "I-"

"Shouldn't you be wandering around, finding some man you want me to seduce on your behalf? Not to brag, but I'm pretty good at getting friends laid." He laughs.

I'm tempted to, but he has me all kinds of distracted with how shifty he is. Gunner loves surprising people, I know that. He's also all about enjoying a moment when he sees an opportunity.

"I'm focused at the moment." I follow his look to the entrance. "You have a secret and I want in."

"Of course I do. I have the best secrets. I think you want another drink more, though." He stares at my glass for a while. "Gin tonic."

With that, he's up and headed toward the open bar. I'm not going to like whoever is going to join us at the table. He's made that clear, or he'd be bouncing in his seat, excited beyond belief and unable to keep it to himself. I just have to put the hints together. He said something about familiar faces. But he doesn't know my friends and other than Sophie's three other husbands, I don't know his.

So, I would have only met them at the few things we've done together. Holden's birthday party or the wedding. That limits things pretty intensely.

Something uncomfortable pricks at my brain. I bite my thumb nail for a second, then I get it. It's so obvious. I swallow hard and shoot a glare in Gunner's direction. He raises a glass to me with that damn smirk on his face. Three people come to mind and it's a big, intimidating, overwhelming hell no.

HUNTER

"Is that Valerie?" I ask, nudging Chase.

He follows my gaze to the girl with dark hair and a sexy black dress. Cleavage on display, full-back showing tempting skin, the frustrated purse of her lips.

"Doesn't look like the Valerie I left at the wedding," He says smugly.

I elbow him hard. He's made it inescapably clear that he fucked her, twice. I got the first kiss, but he got the home run. Lief joins us while pocketing his phone. "We good?"

"Got the all-clear." He agrees. "I'm on call."

"Dad should be able to survive one night without us." I snort. "As good as we are, we should still be allowed a weekend off."

"Slacker," Chase says. "No wonder I get the better assignments."

There's no point in trying to correct him. He's dick deep in 'little brother' syndrome. Always has something to prove, but can be a manipulative little shit too. Leif goes to the silent auction, moving through people like a shadow. I make my way to the bar with my brother in tow. He would never admit it, but he hates situations like this.

He's a chameleon, Gemini that he is, but would much rather be one-on-one with every single person in the world instead of at an event where he can't know everything happening at the exact moment it happens.

Once we have our drinks, I spot Gunner with Valerie and head their way. Gunner meets our eyes, hair messy, eyes tired, tie a little cocked.

"If I didn't know better, I'd say you haven't slept in weeks," I greet.

He stands up and pats my back in a one-armed hug. "Nah, just waiting for the baby."

Chase gives him a fist bump and sits one chair over from Valerie. She's giving me a 'fuck off' face, but then takes a healthy drink. "Gunner, should I bother to look at the prices?" She asks.

"Put my name down for a spa weekend," He encourages her.

She starts to walk away, but I cut her off. "Long time no see, gorgeous. Did you miss me?"

"Haven't thought about you once. It's Hank right?"

"You wound me." I pat my chest. "I know you haven't forgotten my name, Valerie."

"So much faith in subpar kissing and basic dance skills." She skirts by me that easily.

Every step she takes confirms she belongs on a runway. Her head held high, like no one in the room deserves eye contact and their judgment doesn't mean a damn thing to her, the sway of her hips. All of it makes me want to tame her.

Something about the chase turns me on. I've had too many girls throw themselves at me. It's easier, but I learned early that the easy things aren't the best things in life. Earning a win is so much better than having it handed to me.

"You're drooling," Chase announces.

I wipe my mouth reflexively and sit by Gunner. He's balancing every drink of bourbon with water. He nudges me. "Don't look at me like that."

"Like what?" I smirk.

"Like I've lost my fun." He takes some of the hors d'oeuvres offered. "I haven't. I'm just not willing to embarrass myself tonight. Not with my wife at home waiting for me."

"You need to get laid," Chase chimes in. "Always does me good. Makes me more fun to be around."

My eyes flick around the room quickly. No matter where we are, I feel the pressure of maintaining control. If any competitors or rivals are here, I'll need to check in. I'm hoping there aren't, just to make for an easier night of seducing Valerie, but being sure is more valuable.

"You look constipated." The woman herself says.

Lief stands by her side like it's an accident. I stand and brush a lock of hair from her face. "Are you worried about me, sweetheart?"

"Just wanted to prepare in case tonight was going to be *more* uncomfortable."

I lean forward to whisper in her ear. "You didn't seem too uncomfortable wrapped around me at the reception, even when I whispered my plans for the night in your ear. All that is still on the table by the way."

"If I wanted it, I wouldn't have waited this long to see you again." She pats my chest.

I see her eyes drop to my chest and then lift back to my face. That's right, baby, I'm all muscle. I'm no stranger to dedication and I'd make sure she had a good time, was satisfied in every possible way, would lose her voice screaming my name and begging for more.

Goosebumps prick her skin and I see her pulse thudding in her throat. I put my hand over hers. "If you want to sample something other than the food, let me know. I'm pretty tasty too."

She scoffs and jerks her hand away, taking her original seat. I'm not at all surprised that Lief sits next to her. He's sweet on her, despite not saying a word. Not her name, not any reference to her. His conversation is all work and fun facts from research he's done, or basic pleasantries.

"I bet you fifty they talk about the weather again," Gunner says when I sit. "Just like their first conversation."

I take the bet and we listen in. Lief hasn't ever met a conversation he wants to start, but Valerie shivers. "Not enough whiskey at this event to melt the snow outside."

"Nearly done. We're in March now." Lief says. "Although, there have been recorded years where it's lasted into April."

"May further north," Valerie says. "Did you know seasonal depression is most pronounced in winter in part due to the snow and overcast weather?"

I pay up and shake my head. The ice in my drink has more interesting conversations when they bump into each other. I nudge Gunner. "Make sure that goes toward fun and not ..., diapers."

"We'll see." He chuckles. "Maybe I can convince Sophie to go out on a date."

"You'll need it," I say.

There's a dance floor and I'm about to try my luck asking Valerie to dance, but my brother beats me to it. She takes her time accepting, watching him carefully, then finally slides her delicate hand into his.

They follow the unspoken code of slow, appropriate dancing and I roll my eyes. Why my father sent us here, I don't know. Heading to bars, enjoying clubs, any of that would have been better. This is too stuffy and conservative. The only fun that we could have would be destroying the ho-hum with some actual life.

"You *do* look constipated. Something I don't know," Gunner says. "I was relying on you to make me feel alive, or at least give me a good story."

"Oh, work is fun," I assure him. "Lots of action, a whole lot of things I can't talk about because of the NDA, and you should have seen the vixen I brought home two weeks ago. She didn't leave for two days."

"Your house or the bed." Gunner smirks.

I clink my glass with his. "House. We made sure to break in just about every room."

"Can you confirm, Lief?" Gunner asks, trying to rope him into the conversation.

"The maids are effective, but I wouldn't recommend a blacklight test." He answers.

I chuckle. Lief's lips curve up at the corner, then his eyes flick to the dance floor. I'm not in the habit of telling my friends what to do, but he seriously needs to make a move on Valerie.

I offered her all of us, to give her exactly what Sophie has. She could have all three of us focused utterly and completely on her pleasure and we have plenty of ways to give her that. Pleasure, pain, and everything in between that just makes fucking better.

But Lief is Lief. Even if I did tell him to ask her to dance, he'd shrug, or insist that it's rude to make the first move. That's what you get from a guy who grew up in the Netherlands, Norway, and Denmark. Luckily, he met us in college so he's not completely hopeless.

Valerie and Chase come back and she continues standing, looking at Lief. She asks, "Dance with me."

Not even a question. He stands and follows her to the dance floor. I smirk into my drink. I bet she'll ask Gunner to dance too. She thinks she's teaching me some kind of lesson. Please, I can play the long game. I've perfected patience over the years, especially if it means I'll get what I want.

"You're barking up this tree all wrong." Gunner sighs.

I flick my eyes to him. "Calling me a dog?"

"If it barks like a dog, fucks like a dog ..."

I roll my eyes. "You're full of shit."

"Per Sophie, Valerie likes to have an actual conversation, not be hit on. Maybe when she's tipsy she likes the direct come-ons, but I bet if you take it down about seven notches, she'd give you more than sass."

"Who says I don't like her sass?"

"It might get you laid," Chase amends. "But what do I know? Not like I ... oh wait."

"Jesus Christ. When is this charity going to be done?"

They serve dinner in answer and I check my phone quickly. Uncle Dino reminds me to avoid drawing attention but considering all the ass-kissing I see these old rich dudes doing to each other, it won't be hard.

Chase goes to put his name on some things and Gunner does the same, leaving my eyes to wander. There are plenty of hot girls here, but it's hard to tell who's family and who's a smart ex-sugar baby/ new wife. One girl with copper skin makes eyes at me while wrapping her lips around the straw, but I see that huge ring on her finger.

I may be a dog, but this dog doesn't actively jump into a beating. Married women are off-limits. Convincing a girl to leave a relation-

13

ship isn't the kind of hunt I'm interested in. Valerie sits across the table and looks around the crowd, eyes landing on me.

"What kind of rich bitch are you?" She calmly asks me.

"Excuse me?"

"The kind that holds tight to their wallet or the one who flashes the black card just to get a few extra compliments?"

We watch each other for a long while and I smirk slowly. "I don't give a shit about my wallet."

"Ah, that kind of rich." She sits back like something's been confirmed.

"Are you interested in what's in my pocket, or what's in my pants, Valerie?"

She chokes on her drink, wipes under her gorgeous red lips, and spears me with a hot glare. I bite my bottom lip. "I'm just a little curious considering you had no problem rubbing yourself all over me at the wedding, hardon and all."

"I don't give a shit about your money."

"Don't want to be my sugar baby?"

"I don't want to be your *anything*." She hisses. "You treat girls like prizes to be won. Just because I forgot that for one horny, tipsy moment doesn't change what's obvious. I'd be a notch on your bedpost and I'm not interested in that kind of reputation."

"You don't get to have a place in my bed or on my bedpost unless you beg for it, sweetheart," I assure you. "And trust me, I'd make sure you beg before I'd even kiss you."

"I don't beg."

"You would for me. Want me to prove it?" I ask before taking a long drink.

Valerie's face flushes, but she doesn't back down. That defiant gaze, the slight pout to her lips, the way she's breathing hard. I may just have a challenge on my hands.

"I don't *need* anything from you, Hunter. I can get what I *want* from my battery operated friend with the extra perk of not dealing with your attitude."

"When you get tired of fucking yourself and want someone else to do it, call me." I toss her my card and wink. "I expect it'll be soon."

VALERIE

*I*t's not fair that they're this sexy. I figured I just remembered them better than they were but no if anything I downplayed it. If Hunter just had a random mole, or a giant wart on his face or was half as smooth, this wouldn't even be a conversation. I mean … I'm not shallow, but he's my perfect brand of cocky and sexy.

But I won't beg. I didn't beg for Chase, and that's a low blow I won't pull out yet. I know better than to reveal the ace in my hand. So I sit back and sip. Then say, "Honey, if either of us is going to beg, it's gonna be you."

"Not a chance." That bad-boy smile turns up his lips as he glances from my tits to my mouth. "I know what I offer." He gets closer.

"And I know you're dying to fuck me." My lips turn up in a half-smile when his eyes go wide. "I bet I could get you on your knees, begging to taste my pussy, just a single taste. Like a drug you need to get through the next day."

"So I should crawl under the table? That's what you want?"

I wrap my lips around the straw and make sure my cheeks hollow out as I take a long drink, draining the whole glass. His Adam's apple bobs in his throat and his eyes darken. Two can tease. When I lean back, I stroke a lock of hair, brushing my fingers over my cleavage.

"What do *you* want Hunter?"

Because wording matters with him, I can tell. He wants me to admit I'm interested. It's a game to him. But now he's set a bar. I'm not going to beg, he says he never will, so we're at an impasse.

"Are you two playing nice?" Gunner asks, sitting next to Hunter.

"I could be nicer," Hunter croons.

Chase sits back down and stretches. "I bid on a dinner cruise. If I win, would you like to join me, Valerie?"

The direct request takes me off-guard after the verbal sparring with Hunter. My eyes go to Chase and hold. "A date?"

"Why not? Unless you're taken."

Damn, I haven't been on a date, a real date in a *very* long time. Hitting the year mark since I met up with someone with romance in mind other than a quick lay. Because dating is hard when I'm married to school.

I nibble my bottom lip. "It would be hard. I'm trying to study for a big test right now while I'm planning my dissertation and keeping up with classes. "

He cocks his head to the side. "I don't think I asked what you were studying. We were too busy doing other things."

There's the dig I was waiting for. I don't mind being the object in a game of tug of war between them, but I don't want to be a pawn. And I want him to work harder than he did the first time.

"Psychology," I say. "I'm working on my Ph.D., hence the limited time."

"But you came out tonight," Chase presses. "Can I convince you to give me just two hours?"

"Cute." I pat his hand. "I came here as a favor to this over-exhausted mess and his wife."

Gunner nods. "Can confirm. Sophie was worried I'd just pass out in the hotel if I didn't have someone to meet here."

"We're not good enough company for you, Gun?" Hunter asks, completely distracted.

They both focus on him, so I can head to the bar. I stumble and feel strong arms catch me. Turning my head, I see Lief. Now, if this one asked me on a date, I'd be torn. Because I'm pretty convinced Hell itself would have to freeze over for that, but I also think that Lief would be an amazing time.

"Thank you," I murmur.

"Water?" He suggests.

I nod. "It's your friends driving me to drink."

"Alcohol is a poison, Valerie." He reminds me softly with his gruff voice.

Oh god, his voice is a drug itself. How have I not tasted him yet? I shiver slightly under his gaze. His face is so … closed off. Like he's never met an emotion he wants to show. Maybe it's the alcohol or how different he is, but I'm feeling confident.

"Do you *like* dancing with me, Lief?"

He dips his chin once.

"You should *ask* me to dance then. Girls like for men to show interest." I hint.

He hands me my water, but I suck from the straw while he holds it for me. The condensation rolls over his hand and his eyes don't leave mine. I slide my fingers over his and the mix of hot and cold is wild.

"What else would you like doing with me?"

"Getting you sober." It's such a simple answer, so clear cut, no flirting at all.

I continue to watch him, trying that psychology hack, but he studies my face instead, taking me in. I waver on my heels and Lief wraps his arm around me. I swear the man has to be half-robot with strength like this. It's like there's steel under his skin.

"Dancing is hard when drunk. Flirting is easy," He murmurs.

"Talking from experience?"

"No. Observation."

"Observing is good. The best way to know what to expect from people."

"Sometimes." He qualifies.

"Going to school me on psychology?"

Shaking his head very slightly, he pulls me to the side. "I read that a person is what they do and why they do it. Action and motivation," He says.

"I've heard you can tell the character of someone by how they act when they have nothing to gain, what they do when no one is looking," I hum.

"What do you do when no one is looking, Valerie?"

"Depends on the day." I smile.

He considers that and then taps the bottom of my water. I drink it obediently. We say next to nothing as we sit together and I hate that I still don't know where his mind is. The simple, everyday psychology hacks aren't getting me anywhere and I'm not sure what to do with him. Which excites the shit out of me. This never happens. Most men are so predictable.

Even Roman would give *something* if I fished carefully. Lief isn't even *that* open. I cross my legs and look out over the crowd with him. There's a girl that's obviously interested in Hunter, despite the ring on her finger, and she's making her way over slowly, finding people to talk to along the way, things to distract her so it almost seems accidental.

A more brazen blonde drapes herself in Gunner's lap after faking a fall. He's so tired, he doesn't realize it's a come-on – sets her back on her feet – then continues his conversation without giving her a second look.

I smirk slightly. "He's a good one."

"Gunner?" Lief asks.

"I don't know if it's that he's tired or that devoted to Sophie. To avoid a setup that obvious, he must be distracted."

"I see." Lief takes a drink from his glass.

Our silences are normally comfortable, but now I'm overthinking like crazy. "What do you think of meteorology?"

"Not everything that ends in 'ology' is a science." He murmurs. "Like Astrology."

"Oh no. You're telling me astrology's not something you believe in. That everyone in the world falls into one of twelve categories? What a shock." The sarcasm flicks off my tongue "What sign are you?"

"Scorpio." He says.

"Makes total sense then. I'm an Aries. Celebrating my birthday in two weeks," I say simply. "Scorpio … they're normally discreet and secretive. Fearless and bold, but more on the mysterious side. I think there's something about loyalty and passion, but they like stability and routine."

He turns his icy eyes on me and I have the feeling he can read my mind, see through all the bullshit, and to something much deeper than I want him to know.

"Does it fit?" I ask.

"In some areas," He responds.

I laugh and see the corner of his mouth tick up. Maybe he's not completely hopeless when it comes to showing emotion. I take his hand and stroke a few lines. "I bet if I could read your palm it would tell me more about you."

His fingers close around my hand. "Better not to. I believe most women find mystery attractive."

"It's intriguing. There's a difference. Lief." I stand up, feeling a bit steadier than before. "I can't leave Gunner alone too long. Best friend code."

"I see. I appreciate our conversations."

"Almost a compliment." I clink my ring against my glass. "Bravo."

"You look … very nice." He says so softly, that I think I've misheard him.

"And a real one. Thank you," I bend down slightly, hesitate, then press my lips to his cheek. "You look sexy in a suit."

With that, I walk back to our table, not wanting to see the lack of expression on his face. When I sit beside Gunner, I see his energy flagging. I pat his thigh. "Come on, Gun, you're the life of the party."

"Pregnant wife, red-eye, charity event, and you." He lists on his fingers. "A recipe for sleep."

"I'm not that bad." I insist.

But Gunner is struggling. I think of Sophie at home, the way she vents to me, the frustration she feels. Time to clue Gunner in.

"Hey. I'm … pitying you, so I'll give you some tips with Sophie," I offer.

He perks up immediately. I tell him to bring her home things she's been craving before she can ask, to spend time with her like he did before she was pregnant, and not to hesitate being close and involved and giving her plenty of massages and post sexy time cuddles.

He nods and I see him taking mental notes. I grab his arm before he can text her. "Most important, best tactic, if all else fails."

His eyes are glued to me.

"Stand behind her and lift her belly a little, not a jerk or anything, but it will remove some of the weight from her shoulders and make her feel good. You can also say you want to try something you saw online that will make her feel better," I instruct.

He nods. "And that will work?"

"If nothing else works, that last one will. She's carrying around that baby all the time, and I'm sure it's killing her back."

He kisses my cheek. "You are a peach."

"Now put on a smile, lean toward me, take a picture, and send it to her so she knows you've been a good boy."

Gunner does just what I say and we get a picture of Sophie cuddling a pillow. Gunner huffs. "She's not allowed to look that cute and … sexy."

I chuckle. "As if anything could change how hot you think she is."

"Yeah." He nods and grins a dopy smile. "She's amazing. I can't believe how fearless she is about all this while I'm stressing over every baby book."

"You?" I snort and wave my hand dismissively. I know how to boost confidence. "Please, you were in battle. Plus, you've dealt with an angry Roman and even Sophie's dad. A crying baby won't be an issue."

Before the conversation can continue, the announcer taps the microphone and I sit back in my chair. Finally, we can get through the flashing of funds and move on with our night. Hopefully, fingers crossed.

Which means I can escape these brothers who are desperate to one-up each other by having me, and Lief, who is so confusing, go back to my bed like a good girl and rub one out before returning to my pile of textbooks.

God, I have a boring life. My eyes flick to Hunter and Chase, then Lief when he sits down. Would it kill me to spice up my life a few notches? I could tease a little, maybe have someone else do the satisfying for a while?

One trip to hell and back? The price is, apparently, these three men. And considering how they're all glancing at me, I may just be the winner of this specific raffle.

CHASE

*V*alerie keeps looking between the three of us like we're a study. I sit a little taller, try to keep my focus on the stage, and will myself not to think about her naked.

Despite having some fun since our last liaison, I can't quite get her out of my head. I'm smarter than to think she wants something more than sex, but I would love another round with her, or even to make it a regular thing.

She's a hell cat in the bedroom and outside it. I remember her nails dragging down my back, the way she loved to be on top, how she took as much as she gave and never settled for just being present, letting me do all the work. She was in to it.

Plenty of girls I've been with only stay on top for five minutes, then want me to do the rest of the work, but in every position we tried, she was an active participant. And she's good at what she does. Like she's competing against the whole roster of women I've ever met, let alone touched.

I shift in my seat, trying to hide my steadily hardening cock. Okay, I just have to think of Hunter, of Dad, of work and it will go down.

Gunner wins the spa tickets, four for an all-day experience, with a smile and a wave.

He sits back down and takes a drink of the Red bull he got. No alcohol. If this is what married life looks like, I'm not interested. Hunter checks his phone for the fifth time and I feel mine vibrate.

I switch to the Russian keyboard easily. All work communication is in Russian. Without fail. Every time. I tell Dad I'll be back in touch tomorrow, since I can't do anything he needs from my phone, especially at an event.

I know he'll complain about it later. He always does. We're just dogs at his beck and call, expected to jump when he gives the word and do it without a treat. I bite the inside of my cheek to keep the other thoughts at bay.

Now's not the time or place for them.

I win the dinner boat thing, collect my winnings, and look to Valerie again. She mouths 'maybe' to me and I accept that as it is. She has no problem saying no.

As much as I want to pick her brain, find out more about her, find out what makes her tick and why she's so damn aggressive in everything she does, I know that there are more important things in life than a girl.

Not to say anything bad about women, they're wonderful, loving, nurturing – so I've heard, but they're people. They can leave. They can change their mind at any point, even if you've fallen for them completely, even if you've gotten to the point that you love them, they can just be gone in a second and not care about whatever broken mess they leave behind.

Work, even if questionable, won't just walk away from me. I have control there. I have measurable success, and I know that I'm good at what I do, with or without praise. Though I doubt it would kill Dad to recognize it.

25

Hunter nudges my knee and taps his phone against his knee.

I check mine discreetly and see our group message. Lief spotted fucking Stefan. I'm not shocked, Stefan loves these events. Loves to show off power and money, even if he doesn't buy a damn thing.

"Nine." Lief texts.

My eyes flick in that direction and I see him with two girls on his arm. He's telling a story and ignoring the announcements as the girls giggle, touch and stroke him, nibble his ear, and hang all over him. He thinks he's some kind of fucking King just because of his rank.

He should be taken down a peg before he starts to get reckless and gets ideas about what he can get away with in *our* city. His father knew his place. Stefan will learn his. By tripping over his ego and falling on his face, or with some help.

Once the announcements are done, we're encouraged to drink and dance and enjoy the food they've prepared for the event. I stir my drink with the swirl of my hand. Food is probably a good choice.

I get up, then turn to Valerie. "Want anything, gorgeous?"

"Sure." She smiles and glances over. "Whatever you like I'll like."

That challenge in her eyes, the way she leans forward just enough, holds my eyes a second longer than necessary, smiles coyly, it's a distraction and I *know* she knows it. But it doesn't change that I make her plate, trying to pick out the best items available. Hunter nudges me.

"You're letting her walk all over you, man, have I taught you nothing?"

"How to drive women away?" I shoot back. "Are you forgetting who got to fuck her?"

"Just keep throwing that in my face." He snorts. "She's interested or she wouldn't go back and forth with me." He growls.

"She's interested in the easiest way to slit your throat," I grumble.

The server jumps a second and I smile. "Sorry, brother talk."

He nods, gives a short laugh, and moves on. The comment earns me another elbow in my side. Hunter uses his growly 'I'm in charge voice', "be careful saying things like that."

"Come on, no one believes that level of violence. It's always a joke."

To the people outside our family, anyway. There's a time and place for things and I've learned it well. I know how to blend in as needed, how to be the most likable person in any room. Hunter just throws himself around expecting people to fall in line.

"Look, little brother, I just don't want any issues to arise. I don't need to save your ass again."

"I haven't asked you to fight for me in years," I mutter.

Not since I learned how to bring a person to heal verbally. Threats go a lot farther than fists if you can find the right spot to attack. And I've made it a fucking art form. Especially with everyone's data being online and doxing being so easy. Find the right coding and then everything in the world wide web opens up with the minimal need for passwords.

That said, my brother has gone to bat for me. He used to jump into whatever circle-jerk of guys decided to jump me in middle school and take the blows, take the victory, and the detention that followed.

Even now, it's strange to see him without a bruised face, a bloody nose, or a split lip, Once our plates are full, we walk back to the table. Hunter smiles at a pretty brunette and keeps his voice low. "Can you check Stefan's social media at the moment?"

"He keeps his pages public. Won't be hard. Won't tell us much."

"We can turn it into a game with the psychology student and see what she can pull from it."

Rolling my eyes, I stand behind Valerie and set the plate in front of her. I stroke over her bare arms and lean forward so she'll feel my breath across her skin, just like when I fucked her from behind. "Is that satisfying, babe?"

"Very." She says, looking back at me, she rewards me with a soft, lingering kiss to my jaw. "Thank you, Chase."

I still feel a buzzing in my skin when I sit down. We eat slowly and I check Stefan's page. He's grumbling about having to do the marketing side of work, then sends out a very positive message about the charity ball and how 'honored' he is to have been invited and how eager he is to add to his father's legacy.

"So, psychology, Valerie? That's a big field." I start.

"My master's degree is in clinical psychology. In undergrad, I got really into a TV show about FBI profilers and thought it would be fun, but now I'd rather help individuals get through things." She shrugs.

"So you can diagnose all our issues?" Hunter asks with a smirk.

"Sure, narcissist." She bats her eyelashes easily. "But it wouldn't be ethical for me to do that without a sit-down conversation and something tells me you don't have that patience."

I try to hide my smile by stuffing my mouth. Gunner inhales his food, then turns to Valerie. "You don't come across like some nerd who evaluates people."

"There's a professional life and a fun life. If I spent all day evaluating people, I'd never have a conversation that would go anywhere." She sets her fork down thoughtfully. "It's hard to fully separate though when you can recognize what you're studying in others."

"Yeah?" I ask.

"Tell me about me." Gunner encourages.

She holds his gaze for a long time. "I can't."

"Why!" He demands.

"It's no fun if I tell you. I'd rather watch you chase your tail." She continues eating. "Plus, I already gave you Sophie hacks."

"Fair." He slumps a little.

She watches him a moment longer, then sighs. "You're a people pleaser. Making jokes, being the life of the party, it makes others happy and you know it. You run around to make everyone else happy, then crash before you know what to do with yourself."

He considers that for a moment and lights up. "As long as it's working!"

She laughs and shakes her head.

"So, what would you say if someone complained on social media about having to do something mundane, then posted about this charity and how meaningful it is and how they want to protect a legacy."

"That's obvious, even to someone who's not a psych major. Next." She dismisses.

My eyes go to Lief. He needs to pull some weight with this and if he and Valerie can talk about the weather, the most mundane and cliché topic in the world, he can get her to talk about this.

"He'd like to validate his thought with a professional," Lief comments.

Valerie takes a slow breath. "The first post, which if they're a public figure will probably be removed soon by a P.R. team says it all. This event is an obligation that they don't have an interest in. They're keeping up appearances and protecting a legacy is different than building one, so if they're just protecting it, they don't have a personal stake in the matter, just the ... need to make others believe they care."

Well, that second part wasn't fucking obvious. She waves her hands like glitter should fall from her fingers. "What do you three do?"

"We work for the same company." I hedge.

"I do security and investigations." Lief volunteers, a steep simplification that borders on a lie.

"I manage online accounts." Another close lie from me.

"Oh, Valerie, are you curious?" Hunter gives her his shit-eating grin. "I'd be happy to tell you as post-sex pillow talk."

"Your job must be boring then." She says before finishing her plate. "Good talk guys, almost nice to see you again. Gun, let's get you to your hotel and some much needed sleep."

"Oh come on, the life of the party can't leave," I say loud enough that I'm sure Stefan hears.

"Don't make me pull the mom voice." Valerie threatens, one hand on her hip. "You have a flight early in the morning, Gunner."

"Yeah." He nods. "Responsible Reba here is calling the shots."

"How are you this pussy whipped to Val without getting pussy?" Hunter snorts.

The glare Gunner shoots him should work like a bullet, dropping Hunter to the ground into an unconscious daze. Valerie takes care of that quickly. "The same way you're a dick when yours gets no attention."

"Oh, it gets plenty."

"Not the right kind if you're still coming on to me." She snaps. "Come on, Gun."

VALERIE

"*T*hanks." Gunner murmurs once we're outside. "Normally I'm better with comebacks, but ... I'm off."

"I know." I pat his arm. "Why do you think your wife called in back up?"

"She's a damn wonderful wife, that's why." He laughs. "Knows I need some taking care of at events like this or I'd run in circles, just like you said." He pauses a moment. "You really think that I'm going to be able to be a good husband *and* a good dad?"

"Absolutely," I assure him. "Parenthood is all about learning and you have a whole team to tackle it! With Sophie, just ... keeping being the Gunner she gets all shy and blushy to talk about. The one who reads romance with her and drives her wild and there won't be any issues at all."

"You're not supposed to know about that," He hisses.

"Best friends talk. Get some sleep, as much as you can before your flight."

Thanking me again, he gets in the car and heads out. Before I can make my way to my car, I *feel* someone close. The hair on the back of my neck stands up and goosebumps break out across my skin. I'm being watched.

My hand inches into my purse, ready to mace whoever is stupid enough to approach, but when I glance over my shoulder, I see Lief. I don't know how he appears like he's always existed everywhere at once, but I'm dying for that superpower.

"Yes?"

"I'd like to ask a favor."

I lean my head to the side. "Only if I can call you a Viking without you walking way."

The corner of his mouth twitches again. "Is it okay if I were to contact you if I have questions about potential business clients? If I feel something might be off?"

"You realize I don't have my Ph.D. and I'm not licensed to consult, right?"

"I do. It would be … informal."

"Is this how you ask to go on a date?"

"No!" He trips over the simple word, then clears his throat. "Strictly professional."

"What a shame, Viking. I'm much more cooperative with food in front of me." I shrug and head toward my car.

"Valerie." He keeps my pace easily. "At least … may I give you my card?"

"Sure." I put out my hand.

He puts it there but keeps walking with me, at ease, glancing around. Security, right. Probably doesn't trust our surroundings enough to let me walk alone in the dark. I tighten my coat around me.

"What kind of perve would be out in winter?"

"Pardon?"

"That's why you're walking me to my car, right? To protect me or something. You know I have pepper spray in my purse. I have sharp nails and sharp teeth too." I've never needed protecting and I'm not interested in some silent bodyguard who won't make a move.

Lief's hand brushes mine, just the softest skin-on-skin contact, then he takes off his coat and puts it around me. I blink in surprise, nearly trip over the curb, and end up in his arms. His eyes widen as he gently picks me up and sets me on the sidewalk.

"You need protection from your own feet."

"And you must be freezing without your coat," I whisper, not letting go of his arms.

"I grew up in cold. This is nothing. Spring weather."

"Tell me more."

"Europe."

I roll my eyes. "We need to work on the quality of your answers if we're going to be working together, Lief. One word doesn't tell me much about anything."

He swallows and I take that as my cue to continue walking to my car. I get to it and shake while unlocking the door. I offer him his coat, but he motions to the car. "It will take time to heat."

"You know, here it's normal that if a guy walks a girl to her car and she's made it obvious she's interested, she'd get a kiss." I huff. "I have a feeling, that's not on the agenda for tonight."

It takes three tries for my car to start. I crank the heat, then stand up. Lief just watches me, his eyes are churning. "You're interested in me?"

"It's pretty fucking obvious to everyone but you. You're hot, mysterious, have a ton of fun facts that make me want to go home and research other topics, and you play hard to get really well."

"You slept with Chase," He says it simply and the wall goes right back up over his eyes.

"Because you walked away!" I force myself to lower my voice. "And I'm sure you haven't been celibate your whole life or slept with someone because you wanted to because you were happy and horny and wanted to feel someone else against you instead of your hand."

I take a chance and close the space between us. After trying to gauge his expression, I carefully touch his chest. "If me fucking your friend after giving you the green light means you're not interested, the decent thing to do is to tell me so I don't …"

"Don't what?"

"Nothing." I glance at my car, willing it to warm faster.

He sighs and turns my chin to face him. "I do appreciate stability and routine. I like working because it is clear and defined. People, no matter how many books I read, do not make sense."

"Which is why you want me to check out your clients, I get it."

He releases my chin. "All people, Valerie. Not just clients. I enjoy our conversations, even when you are … assuming things."

"I wouldn't have to assume if you'd tell me."

His lips definitely curl up this time. He leans toward me. "Where's the fun in that?"

A shiver that has nothing to do with the light flurry of snow teases my spine. Lief tightens his coat around me. "Return it to me when we go over a client. You need it more than I do."

34

"Definitely a Viking," I grumble.

He stands there another moment, makes sure I get in my car, then carefully closes the door. I roll down my window and look him over again. "I don't get how you are friends with those two. You're so different."

"In some ways more than others." He says calmly. "Drive safely."

With that he turns and heads back inside, shoving his hands in his pockets as he goes. I just noticed his long hair is tied in a bun at the back of his neck, just noticed that he didn't bother with a tie, just noticed that I'm clutching his card like it's a lifeline in the ocean.

These three are definitely going to be taking up real estate in my head.

I get home, strip myself of my dress, and flop in bed, stretching out. Since I'm feeling particularly sexy, I take a few selfies, showing off my tits and the simple rose tattoo under my right breast.

Wrapping my arm over my breasts to hide all but the top and bottom curls, I take another picture. Before I can do anything more, I get a text. The notification introduces the strange number as Hunter, which means Chase gave him my information.

I open it and ask him what he wants.

HUNTER: waiting for you to beg, beautiful. Ready now that you're all alone?

VALERIE: I have what I need to be satisfied. Night.

I hesitate a moment, then put Lief's number in my phone. I toss it to the side and reach in my nightstand for my vibrator. I stare at it for a moment, then turn it on a low setting, low on my belly, thinking of all three of the men, even though I hate it.

Hunter kissing me, because, despite everything, he's damn good at it, Chase kissing and licking my nipples. His mouth is so much better than my fingers stroking and pinching. And Lief, just watching,

35

hungry churning his gaze on my body as his friends make me moan and pant.

My thighs squeeze together as I imagine him approaching, guiding my underwear down my legs, and pushing my thighs apart. I finish stripping, then press the head of the toy against my clit, rubbing slowly, imagining Lief's fingers there, working and teasing me, winding me up without any promise of more.

"Fuck." I pant as my hips rock forward.

Hunter would pull away to watch, tell me if I want to be fucked, I have to beg. But I don't beg. Chase would be more convincing, layering soft bites and soft kisses across my chest while Lief would give me a hint of what I could have, dipping the tip of his finger inside me, just to go back to my clit.

"You'll beg. Soon." Hunter's voice fills my head, all those naughty unsaid promises.

Cocky, but I'm sure he'd be willing to tie me up and watch me squirm if it means he gets what he wants. Would he spank me? Would he gag me? How naughty would he get? I moan and up the vibration setting another notch.

My hips rock against it as I tease myself, running it from my clit to my entrance and back. Just like Lief would tease me. Hunter would order me to beg for satisfaction, for him to fuck me while I blow Lief, challenge me to take even one of their cocks, let alone two.

Lifting my toy, I wrap my lips around it, stilling the vibrations as I taste myself on the silicon. It's not quite as satisfying as Chase's cock was. Doesn't make my mouth water, doesn't slide perfectly across my tongue and down my throat, but it's damn good, especially when I keep using my fingers on my pussy.

Lief would give me two of his big fingers, pushing them in and curling them right against my g-spot. I moan around the toy.

Hunter would be able to smell the victory. "Such a good girl. Don't you want to use that mouth to beg? Don't you want to come?"

My head drops back and I nod. "Fuck yes, I do."

Then I break the fantasy and fuck myself like I need to. By the time I come twice, my arm is sore, my thighs are soaked, and I'm a panting shaking mess. A little laugh escapes as I look at my ceiling.

"Fuck you, Hunter. I don't need to beg to come."

But as I clean up in the shower, then make my bed with new sheets, I look at my phone and see another text from him.

HUNTER: You'll be a good girl for me soon, wet, begging, and submissive.

The devil emoji finishes it.

Honestly, this is the kind of text I'd find creepy as hell if I didn't know that he means it. That he'll wait to make a move until I show interest until I'm tugging him against me and taking what I want, or obeying his every word.

It's a game. Which means I'm going to win.

But maybe I should go another round with my battery-operated boyfriend before I take on this challenge. If I'm satisfied from the start, it'll be easier to be the one in charge, right? I'll be less likely to cave or even think about caving.

So I finish myself in the shower with the hot water running over my body and smile. He wants a challenge? I'll give him one that he can't win. I'll get through that layer of ego, that fucking cocky mask he has on, and see what's hiding underneath, just so I can see if he's all talk, or can actually do better than Chase.

Game on. I'm playing to win.

LIEF

*S*now clutters the road and sticks to the windshield of our town car. Streetlights keep the car lit as we continue toward home. The radio plays low, too low to make out any of the words. I drum my fingers on my knee and glance to Hunter. He wears a satisfied smile and I know that it's not due to winning anything.

"I have hope for Valerie." He answers the unspoken question. "You may have gotten her first, Chase, but if she really hated me, she just wouldn't answer."

"Not the point of tonight," I say. "Stefan."

"That bastard doesn't belong at any event," Chase agrees. "Although I don't think that Valerie offered much insight."

"We had suspicions that he was not interested in maintaining his father's agreement. I believe she solidified that," I say simply.

"Do you have a thought you don't say?" Hunter chuckles. "Anything that just sits in your head?"

"No." It's sometimes a lie.

After all, when I was standing in front of Valerie and she asked if I was interested, I hedged. I'm very interested in her. I enjoy the way she speaks to me. I enjoy the time she spends getting to know me, her laugh, and I regret not being the one who spent the night with her.

My gaze flicks to Chase. Hunter's more open about his frustration. I don't prefer to linger on jealous thoughts. "I provided Valerie my card."

"Of course you did. That's your classic move when you want to fuck, right? Not just tell a woman you'd like to be on top of her?" Hunter says. "I think that would be easier, especially with your looks."

"She can be an asset when it comes to finding out more about those we are … interested in."

"Oh yes, just invite her to dinner, a meeting, with said person." Chase rolls his eyes. "Put her directly within the business."

That is not the thought. The thought is to utilize her abilities in the best way. If that happens to lead to more time with her, so be it. We return to the main house – the mansion – and find Mr. Volkov.

He adjusts his cuffs and glances up at his sons. "Did you achieve the goal?"

"We behaved." Hunter puts on his normal face for his father.

He is always closed off with his father. Chase has told me that it's the same face he would wear after a fight in high school. Interesting.

"Stefan was there, with women on his arm. Nothing appeared to be off," Chase agrees. "It was a simple night, father."

"Interesting." The Russian tint to his words makes it seem sharper, not that his eyes help. "I was expecting more information."

"What can be gained by being at a charity event?"

"An opportunity is an opportunity!" He growls. "Perhaps I put my faith in the wrong people. I could have sent Ivan and Sven. I imagine they would have provided more details, perhaps not been distracted."

"What makes you think we were distracted?" Hunter looks at his nails.

"The fact that you have nothing meaningful to say at any given moment."

Mr. Volkov is not a man who appreciates compromise. Anger is the default for him. He takes a slow breath and smooths his hand over his steadily balding head, then down his face, rubbing his jaw.

"I'm not sure what I need to do to instill the proper respect and discipline into you two. You don't have the luxury of enjoying events like that when you could have spoken to Stefan, you could have gotten us more business by charming eligible ladies instead of simply sitting on your asses and eating."

A harsh judgment considering nothing was said beforehand.

"Instigating Stefan wouldn't have achieved anything. Better to make our appearance known and wait for him to reach out." I say calmly. "He is predictable."

Mr. Volkov looks at me, then sneers. "Anything else to say, Lief?"

"We did make necessary connections."

He considers this, then nods once. "Then I apologize for my outburst. Please. Who is the person who is so important and can assist us?"

Hunter shakes his head at me once. I shrug. "A psychologist who could be an asset if we have doubts about a conflict or person."

"That is positive." His face changes immediately, lighting up with an easy smile. "Then you did wonderful, my boys. "Otlichnaya rabota."

They incline their heads. Mr. Volkov says he is going out and there is vodka to reward their efforts in the freezer. Ivan will be joining him and he will let them know anything they need to know.

Old man doesn't trust them. He's made that clear. He walks out with the large, muscular Ivan trailing behind. Hunter goes to the freezer while Chase grabs three glasses. The kitchen is ornate, never an issue considering all the appliances are new and everything is kept sparkling clean for fear of Mr. Volkov.

"Even those poor cute maids are afraid of Dad." Chase snorts. "If Uncle Sergei hadn't prepared us for him, we would have had a different time."

"Doesn't matter. A dick is a dick. No wonder Mom …" Hunter trails off and glances at his brother before pouring the Vodka. "I'm still against us getting Valerie involved in our shit."

"Agreed," I say simply, even though I'm sure I wouldn't act on any order.

"And dragged an innocent girl into Father's attention." Hunter snarls. "She may be a sassy woman who can hold her own, but being involved in this family and this … business isn't an *optional* thing. The second she enters, she's in it for life. Do you know what that could do to her?"

Chase rubs his forehead. "The second she knows anything or Dad thinks she knows anything, she's going to be in trouble. Then she's only good for as long as she's useful."

"Your father mentioned there being a potential informant in the business." I remind them as I take my own drink and sip from the glass. "We can ask what to look for without involving her further"

"That's bullshit and even you know it, Lief," Hunter says. "Valerie will be curious; she'll insist on being involved somehow."

"No," Chase disagrees. "No, she said she didn't even have time for a date due to her schedule. She'll do everything she can over the phone or email."

"Which will still lead to her!" Hunter takes a slow breath.

"You have your father's temper," I say.

41

"Some thoughts can be inside thoughts. You don't have to share every observation with the world." Hunter huffs.

I shrug.

We finish our half glasses of Vodka and my phone buzzes in my pocket. Pulling it out, I see an unfamiliar number. I open the message and see Valerie's name.

VALERIE: I'm interested in the offer. Don't have much time though. Bribe me with dinner or it's all over email.

"She confirmed Chase's statement," I say.

Hunter shakes his head, but gives up, storming away. Chase shrugs. "Have a good night. A free night. No … shenanigans."

I head to my room, shut the door, and get through a shower in the ensuite bathroom. In bed, I respond to Valerie.

LIEF: Email is preferred.

VALERIE: You on top of me is actually preferred.

She's brazen, doesn't hide what she wants. But, as Hunter stated, it is better that she not be involved. Which means keeping our distance from her, especially on our own turf.

The week passes and I find myself standing near the college, leaned up against a building, looking at my phone to blend in. Smoking used to be the best option, from what I've heard.

I glance at the picture of my target, then glance around. Wanted for questioning. A simple snag and bag mission.

When the man walks around the corner, the scar on his face, a perfect match to the photo, same dark eyes, same hat even, I tap his shoulder.

"Do you know how to get to American University?"

"Sure, it's just down that road. You're close." He points.

When his eyes leave me, I twist him around, hit the necessary button on my phone, then inject the sedative I hid up my sleeve. He stumbles slightly, and I support his weight. "You should lay off the alcohol, friend."

The car pulls up and I thank another pedestrian for helping me to get him into the vehicle. We draw a bag over his face once in the safety of the tinted car and Sven nods to me. "Never an issue with you, Lief."

"My job is simple," I say.

We bring the man to the mansion and down to the basement. Sound-proofed, sectioned off for an interrogation room, some holding facilities, and a room I prefer not to think about. I drop the man into the interrogation room, use a zip tie on his arms, so he is stuck to the chair. Bolted into the floor, as I suggested.

Leaving him in the locked room, I get Mr. Volkov. He arches an eyebrow at me as I pull him from his meeting in the smoking lounge he likes to use to entertain guests. There are three unfamiliar male faces.

"Mr. Erikson, how can I help you?"

"Your package has been delivered. Is anything else required of me tonight?"

"I'd like you to sit in with me. Have Hunter join my guests, they're from the motherland and shouldn't be left alone for long."

I text Hunter as I follow. Mr. Volkov down to the basement. I stand behind the man as instructed as Mr. Volkov sits. Pulling the canvas bag off his head, he sputters and groans.

"Now, Mr. Smith." Mr. Volkov folds his hands. "My sources tell me that you have some … overlapping friends."

"Wha?" He's still under the effects of the sedative.

"Don't play coy, it's unbecoming." Then he nods to me.

43

I wrap my hand around his neck, specifically the untattooed hand, then squeeze, pushing up on his jaw as he struggles against me. When Mr. Volkov nods again, I release the man.

"I don't have time for men who are unwilling to cooperate. Time is valuable … wouldn't you agree?"

"What do … do you want?" The man coughs.

"You see, Mr. Smith, I prefer my secrets and business stay with me until *I* decide otherwise. I'm guessing, if we were to look at your phone, we'd see some contacts I don't approve of. As a very *trusted* member of my company – someone I consider family, I would expect you to understand my position."

"I haven't said anything." He pants. "I only work for the Russians."

"Please." Mr. Volkov motions to me.

Without hesitation, I put a knife to the man's throat, threatening the tender skin there. Mr. Volkov continues. "If you are not with the Volkov's, it doesn't matter where your allegiance is. But your wife will wonder where your body is. Do I make myself clear?"

"Yes!" He scrambles. "Yes! I don't share any information. I don't share the books. Everything is on encrypted files. Your organization is safe! I swear! I would never betray a friend!"

"Am I your friend, Mr. Smith? Do I need to provide more incentive, perhaps?"

Obediently, I dig the edge of the knife into his neck, drawing a trickle of blood that slowly works down his throat to the top of his shirt.

"No! We are good friends! Perhaps you should meet Marcia. My wife is always interested in friends."

Mr. Volkov waves me away.

I wipe off my knife, put it back in my pocket, and place one of the tissues I carry against the man's throat. I am merely a tool. Nothing more. A well paid tool, but I know my place in the business. I know my worth. And as long as Mr. Volkov has enemies, he'll need men like me to solve problems creatively.

"Thank you. You may go."

And I do, heading out and taking care of evidence as needed. My life isn't as pretty as many think. All the more reason not to show interest in Valerie.

VALERIE

"Come on!" Elaine bumps my hip as we walk back from Advanced Social Psychology. "Taking time off from school is important. Self-care. A way to relieve stress, all things that we've learned are vitally important for studying."

"Studying is also vitally important." I giggle.

Elaine is sweet. She loves to have fun and can make just about every lecture exciting. I roll out my neck. "As much as I would love to come out with everyone, I don't have a date."

"You don't have to! I can do a set up for you. I know this guy, Dino, I bet you'd love him." She bounces on her toes.

I don't know. I can't picture myself yelling "Dino" while coming. Even "Hunter" is preferable to that. And it has been a week since I properly teased any of those men. Maybe I'm overdue. A slow smile curves up my face as my stomach clenches.

"If I can get a date, I'll be there. Saturday, right?"

"Of course! We don't do parties on weekdays. None of us are insane."

"At least not certifiable." I laugh.

She cackles and we both grab coffee before parting ways for the day. I stretch and roll my back out at home and commit another sticky note to this party. Six P.M. Saturday for a house party in Elaine's honor.

No messages from Chase, none from Hunter, none from Lief. That won't do. I need some attention. Who better to text than the one least likely to respond. If I go without, I'll get to Hunter, tease him relentlessly and maybe give him a chance to show off exactly what he can do with all that talk.

Or I could message everyone but him and enjoy knowing he's stewing because I won't give him attention and I *know* Chase will tell him if I'm texting him. I grin darkly at the idea.

So I text Lief.

VALERIE: If you're interested at all, I hope you enjoy this.

Then I send the teasing photo I took the night of the charity event, where my arm is across my tits. A girl can't show everything to a guy who might not appreciate it, after all.

I get through studying a bit, then look at my phone.

LIEF: I enjoy it greatly.

VALERIE: Would you want more?

I stare at the phone, but he doesn't answer right away. I grumble to myself and think about that damn fantasy again. I could fully dive into it, even just with Lief. A shiver teases my spine and my phone vibrates again.

LIEF: Of course, I would.

VALERIE: Are you sure? You're not very enthusiastic.

LIEF: Please?

I smile. If that's what he thinks is more enthusiastic, I want to scoff. How the hell does his brain work?

VALERIE: Then you should come to campus on Saturday.

With that question pricking my brain, trying to make me check my phone over and over, or take it back, or anything in between. Maybe I should have started with Chase. He's more predictable. I understand him. I know how to push him in the right direction. I'm sure it would probably be an exchange – if he comes to my event, I go on the dinner cruise with him.

LIEF: I will see.

I stare at the reply. It's definitely not what I expected, but I'm not complaining. Hell no. I'd love to have that regal Viking on my arm, have him confuse my friends, have him throw everyone for a loop with his simple answers, the confidence he says everything with, the fact he's so different from anyone else I've ever met.

He's not going to mark his territory or drape an arm over me while giving 'piss off' vibes to every other guy, he won't sweep me up into a dance, he'll want me to make the first move and to be sure that I'm the one pushing.

Maybe he's not so different from Hunter. I bet Lief would love me to beg for his attention and his affection. He'd love it if I begged for his cock.

Saturday comes quickly and I still don't have a reply from him. I did text Chase a little bit and he was nice and responsive, at times. As I'm getting ready for the day, my phone buzzes. I pick it up without looking at the name and put it on speaker.

I'll have fun with a spam caller today. I'll just teach them the last lesson so I can better learn it and not waste *my* time.

"Hello?" I ask.

"I'm hurt, Valerie." Hunter's purr comes over the phone and takes my breath away. "Texting my brother and not me? Is it because you'd have to be a good girl for me? Not up for that challenge?"

"Maybe it's your personality I'm not up for," I smirk at the mirror anyway.

"And maybe you're afraid to poke holes in my ego because you know you'd like what you'd find under it. Or under my clothes."

I roll my eyes. "Minus two points for that line. Are you capable of talking without flirting?"

"Want to find out?"

I hesitate a moment. "Maybe I'd be more willing to text you if you had an actual conversation with me instead of just trying to get in my pants, playboy."

He considers that as I apply my mascara, making faces at myself.

"We could have a conversation over dinner. There is something non-sexual I'd like to talk to you about."

"And bribing me with dinner?"

"Consider it a favor. And I'd be honored if you'd do me this favor. A face-to-face conversation about an important issue while I can see your reaction … and enjoy your company."

"I'm considering it."

"I bet you are."

"There goes another point." I sigh. "You started at ten for a phone call, if you get to zero, I'm hanging up."

"You don't like my games?" I can hear the smug smile in his voice. "Then why do you keep playing with me, sweetheart?"

Someone says something in the background, but I can't make it out.

Hunter sighs. "Sorry to cut this short, beautiful. I have to go. Let me know when you're available for dinner. The earlier the better."

"Shame, I was going to say right now. But since you're so busy …"

"Woman, don't make me find you and throw you over my shoulder. I will drag you to a restaurant, to bed, or anywhere I want." The growl in his voice gets under my skin in a way that's not entirely unpleasant. "Like the idea of me tossing you around and having my hands on you?"

"Maybe. But I guess we'll never know since you're busy." I hide my growing lust with an easy joke.

He spits out a few curses, then exhales slowly. "Soon."

"Perhaps."

I hang up and shake my head as I stare at myself. I hate Hunter. I hate the kind of man he is and how everything leads back to sex with him. So why am I all flushed, my eyes all dilated, and my pussy wet?

It's just the lack of sex. It has to be. That's all. Once I get a good romp in bed, I'll be cured of this momentary mental slip where I've even considered giving up an ounce of control to a man who will abuse it and leave.

And Hunter will fuck me and leave. I know it in my bones. He's not the kind of guy who would need to have a girl twice because another will come along and catch his attention and start the chase over again.

I let out a harsh breath, go get lunch, then come home for a bit more studying and looking up potential internships I could have. I could work in the prison system, in a treatment facility for those getting twenty-four hour care, or a truly clinical office, seeing patients just like any other counselor.

I like the last option the best. I can learn more methods of care, more intense methods that I've heard of and been curious about based on podcasts I've listened to and researched.

My phone buzzes again and I stare at it. "I am popular today."

I pick it up and wait for someone to speak. After a long time, I hear, "hello?"

"Lief?" I ask.

"Yes." He answers. "I am available. I assume we're going to an event?"

"We are. A party. Are you up for that?" I ask softly.

"I am. Where am I going?"

"I'll send you the address. There's no dress code really, but it's more casual."

"I look forward to it."

"I'll see you soon, then?" I'm still shocked he's coming.

"That sounds like a question, Valerie. Are you having doubts?"

"Listen, you are not the easiest guy to read. Over text, it's even harder so I wasn't sure you'd even be interested. See you in a bit!"

I hang up before my mouth can run away from me. The man is going to get me to spill my soul without any effort at all. I shake my head, make myself focus on reading, then remember I have to text him.

I send him my address, tell Elaine I'm coming, and try to cram some kind of knowledge into my head before teaching it to the one stuffed animal I've kept – a little raggedy bunny that Tristan gave me when I was six.

No girl throws out a present from her big brother, especially when it's protected from so many nightmares. Explaining it to the rabbit helps. That hack I learned from an IT kid I knew in undergrad.

Just as I'm getting ready for the party, putting on a cute, mildly tempting, but not crazy outfit, I get a call from Sophie. I hesitate, then answer the phone on speaker.

"Hey, Soph."

"I love you. I love you. I love you." She sings. "You are wonderful and I'm so glad you went to that gala and talked to Gunner. I owe you a spa weekend."

I laugh. "Which trick worked?"

"The belly lift. Oh god. Oh god. It's so good. Once Gunner did it … well I won't go into the sexy details. Now all my men know the trick and life is pure bliss. I *love* you." "

"I'm glad. I saw it on a whole bunch of videos online and figured if it helped all those women, maybe it would help you."

"I appreciate you so much! Whatever you said … god. You could be a couple's counselor with your skills."

"Damn, I should have you write that down as a recommendation for me soon." I tease. "I'm just glad it helped, especially when I'm too far away to do more."

"Well, you should be receiving some gifts soon. They're thrilled."

"Thank you, Val!" Gunner yells in the background.

I hear Sophie sigh in relief and then take a shuddering breath. "So good."

"He's doing it right now, isn't he?"

She laughs. "Yes. Making me fall in love with him all over again. Hopefully, you can get a weekend soon with some time to spare so we have one last visit before the baby."

"Agreed."

"How are things with the guys?" Gunner asks.

I freeze. Sophie jumps in and asks if he means who she thinks he means and they start placing bets on if I'll fuck them all or one specifically. My cheeks burn. "I don't know what you're talking about."

"Don't hold out on us. I have to live vicariously through you!" Gunner yells.

"Rude." Sophie grumbles.

"I'm not saying a thing. Love you. Bye." I hang up and try to catch my breath. Why am I suddenly shy?

HUNTER

I hate that I can't meet up with Valerie tonight, especially when I know she's holding out on me despite wanting me. But I love a challenge … and being with her will be exactly that. We can't have her around here. It's not safe for her. Our life is pretty and shiny from the outside, with paparazzi following us on slow news days, living in luxury with no concern where our next meal is coming from or if we'll have a house in six months, but that doesn't mean that we don't have our own issues.

Issues and complications that Valerie doesn't need to be a part of. I head downstairs and run into Lief. He has on jeans and a black button-up that's rolled up to his elbows. His hair is down, and he looks comfortable, deceptively.

"Going somewhere?"

"Out."

I pause. "You're not having dinner with Valerie, are you? No business things?"

"None." He agrees, continuing to walk out the door without answering my main question.

Fucker. I head to the conference room near the offices in the back of the house and drop into a chair next to Chase. Being the heir of any business is bullshit when your opinions don't matter, you just get to watch, but this is just an extra helping of that shit.

Maybe, if our mother had stayed around, things would be different. I still remember bits and pieces of her and I can't imagine her staying with dad. She should have taken us with her. Chase is lucky he doesn't remember. It's easier not to know what we had than to keep longing for it.

My father's hand comes down on the table and I jump, thinking of how many times it came down on me when I'd ask when Mom was coming back.

"The Italians can't be trusted."

There are only two other men in the room other than my brother and I. Father said that the more people in the room, the more chances of things getting out. The smaller the meeting, the less risk.

I switch my brain to Russian and fold my hands together on the table while Chase puts on that bored face he keeps for meetings. We're both good at controlling ourselves around Father.

"With Stefan taking over for his father, we have problems. Lorenzo adhered to our ,,, agreement. He played nice, we played nice, a good balance. Let's play this smart so we can limit our involvement outside the community."

The comparatively small Russian community in D.C. has always been Father's main concern. Protecting our people from discrimination, taking care of problems within the community without reaching out to the police, ensuring that we're safe, managed, and have opportunities like any other American citizen.

In that way, at least, he's a good man. Everyone has some redeeming quality. Father makes living in the moral gray area look like internal warfare.

"We can always set up a meeting with Stefan. Your boys are his age." Sven suggests.

My father looks to me, not Chase, me. As the oldest, it's my *honor* and obligation to take care of this. I nod. "We can meet him at a place he'd like and have a conversation that's not likely to be recorded based on venue."

"The more drinks he has, the more talkative he is, and with flashy distractions, he'll spill plenty," Chase agrees.

"We don't need intel; we need an agreement," Father thunders.

I glance to my brother and he shakes his head slightly. Valerie isn't an option. We agree on that. Of course, Stefan would love her. She's sassy and smart, she's clearly someone we're interested in so having any of her attention would make him feel more powerful.

It's an option, but I don't fucking want to take it.

"What?" Father demands. "That look. What is it?"

"Nothing." I wave away. "We can start with a common meeting, showing we are willing to talk, that we see him on equal footing – at least so he believes that, and ask him to do a favor."

"What?"

I studied some basic psychology hacks after meeting Valerie, wondering if she's immune to them and wanting to spot if she tries to use something I can find on Google. "It's something I've seen done in conventional business. Let the person talk about themselves, ask them to do you a favor, certain things will encourage a person to like and trust you more. Once we have his trust, an agreement is easy."

"A true agreement. An understanding that will last longer than his miserable life." Father growls. "Because if Stefan doesn't understand the luxury he has and the power, he will abuse it and get us all in trouble."

"Understood," I say simply.

"One chance. Set it up, see it through, and make it happen. If it doesn't work, whatever you and your brother are hiding will be explored." Father growls, getting closer to me. "Do not disappoint me, Hunter."

He says a few other things, the normal: threats, warnings, orders, then dismisses Sven and the other man. He shuts the door and looks us over. Sitting down, he carefully spreads his hands over the fine wooden desk.

Father believes in appearances, another reason he doesn't want to look at Chase. The rebellious hair, the fact he refuses to wear contacts, he won't blend in or conform. Which is as good as a slap in the face.

"Hunter, I want to be clear."

"You are inescapably clear," I assure, pushing down my urge to include Chase in this.

A big brother protects his sibling. I'd rather take the verbal beating, the physical beating, any and all of it to spare Chase. He can prove himself when it comes to work and I know that, but I have my own duties.

"If this plan of yours doesn't work, I will be … displeased."

Code for pissed; code for violence.

"And whatever the two of you are hiding, if it can help the family …" His eyes go to Chase and I can see him sneer. "No matter the state of the family, I need to be sure you understand that it is more important than any *feeling* you have."

"Understood," I say.

Chase stays silent, just staring at the old man like he's naming each of his wrinkles and scars. When he continues to say nothing, my father hits the table again. "Answer boy. Fall in line."

"What are you going to do? Cut my tongue out?"

I turn on my brother. "You know how important this is. If Stefan doesn't fall in line, the police could get involved, the FBI. Or worse, all out war here in D.C. Is that what you want?"

Chase leans his head to the side.

"There are innocent lives that could get caught in the crossfire. So we will make this option work." I somehow manage to talk through gritted teeth. "You understand *that* don't you?"

"Yes." He whispers, obviously pissed.

I'm going to get an earful later, but that's better than him spilling blood now. Father's meaty hand comes down on my shoulder. "A good son, proving his ability. That is progress, Hunter."

"Chase, get to work checking into the records. We need to know who's reporting our dealings to the locals."

Chase leaves the room obediently and my father focuses all of his attention on me – the last fucking place I want it. I adjust in my chair, sitting taller. He looks me over. "You will be a good man to replace me one day. It is your hesitation that is the problem."

It's not a question, so I don't offer anything.

"I worry that you won't make the hard decisions in the necessary time. The decisions that have no ideal outcome. Someone gets hurt no matter what. I fear that your feelings will stop you from seeing the greater good. Fix that."

"Of course."

"Lief mentioned a psychologist who can help. Perhaps you should book an appointment and get to the root of your attachments. Your indecision."

"Yes, Father."

"I'm giving you an assignment this weekend, best that your brother doesn't know about it." He says before handing me a manila envelope. "Everything you need is there. Make the decision and give Lief the order by Tomorrow night. It's more time than I have for some of my choices."

I don't want to open the folder. I can't. My fingers are numb.

"Prove yourself as an asset or out yourself as no better than Stefan. I name my successor, no matter who it is. If you are not selected, understand the position it will put you in."

I nod and leave with the wave of his hand, stuffing the manila envelope in my jacket. I'm not going to like this choice. I know that. Just like I know if I don't come through, if I'm not named successor, my brother and I will have to leave. I'm sure we could go to New York and that would be far enough, it's dangerous to carry things out if they're not an immediate threat.

Maybe that would be better. If we got the news while my father was alive, we could make the necessary plans. I don't know if Lief would go with us, but it would be easy to get jobs with Gunner, Roman, and them again.

No matter what, we'd survive, as long as the timing is right. But timing is fickle.

In my room, with the door locked, I open the manila envelope. In it is a picture of a man, transcripts of some inconsistencies, and a note that he should be investigated as potentially leaking secrets. Our accountant.

He's been interviewed, but there is still some doubt. Father hasn't given me any options to choose from, but dropping Lief's name has made things clear. He's to be brought back in. For questioning … or taken care of.

Why aren't we having Chase investigate his internet history? So many people send emails, do research, make their plans through their computers now and it could give a clear cut answer. Why are we only taking the old options?

This man has a family, a wife, children, and a grandchild. Not to mention, any kind of murder will draw attention to him, involve the police, and then they will look through his things, which means we will lose our accounts or be investigated as well. Our 'security' firm and 'consulting firm' will be investigated as a part of an innocent attempt to find out who killed the man.

If Lief has been involved once, it's hard to believe that his wife doesn't have suspicions. How much has he told her? Would she need to go too if I put the hit on him?

I scrub my forehead. Father's put the pressure on me, but I have to see this through. I have a brother to consider, a legacy I don't want on my shoulders, Valerie to protect, Lief's trust to maintain, and still my Father, trying to pin strings to me so he can order me around like a puppet.

Groaning, I drop my head to the table, pushing the paperwork to the side. The answer is so easy. I know I'm going to take Chase as the option. I know my father will criticize my soft heart, comparing me to my mother, calling me a flight risk, saying I need to be hardened by the world.

"Fuck!" I hiss. How does Lief do anything he does? "Fuck this. Fuck everything. I should have gone to see her."

I should have. It would have been easier to spend time with Valerie.

There's just too much. I have to simplify. I look at the photo again.

Fuck my father. Fuck his opinions, and fuck his old-school methods. Those methods won't last and I can't believe that murder is the answer. Especially when we could make more money by focusing on the business fronts instead of this ... organization. We'd save expenses, be able to help more of our community, and make drastic *positive* changes.

But what do I know? That's just my soft heart talking.

VALERIE

I just gape at Lief when I see him waiting for me outside. He's sexy as ever and he's actually here. I was sure he'd have some issue, that some *thing* would come up and I'd end up staying in and prepping for my counseling sessions on Monday or studying and explaining more to my stuffed animal.

Lief looks me over and offers me his hand. I take it, savoring his rough palm against mine. "Are you sure you're up for this?"

"I wouldn't be here if I weren't." He assures me, opening the door for me and letting me sit down. "I'm glad you invited me."

"Really?"

"Yes."

With that, he gets in the driver's seat and he follows my instructions to the address Elaine gave me. I chew my bottom lip. Lief studies the road intently, but the silence dragging out is dragging up questions, too many to ask.

"What are you thinking about right now?" I ask, trying for something broad, different from our normal talks.

"The directions you're giving me."

"That's it?"

"I'm simple." He shrugs. "Focused."

"Interesting." I adjust in the seat, so I'm facing him.

If he's a one track mind kind of person, I wonder what he'll be like in bed. Totally focused on me, my body, my pleasure. A shiver teases me. I still haven't gotten a first kiss and I'm already planning on getting even more from him?

"Is this party for something specific?" He asks.

"Fun." I try to hide my laugh. "You know what that is right?"

"I may need a definition." Oh, he's definitely enjoying this.

"I believe in your powers of deduction. And since you like dancing with me, and I assume you like drinking and eating, we'll both have a good time." I motion for him to turn.

Once we get to the party, Lief shoves his hands in his pockets. Rolling my eyes, I stow every thought saying he doesn't want to be here in the back of my mind, and loop one of my arms around his. Those icy eyes pin me for a moment.

"Are you against P.D.A.?" I ask, one eyebrow raised.

"No."

"Then why are you looking at me like I should let you go?"

"That's not what I'm thinking." He says softly. "I'm glad to know you can't read minds."

"Nope. Just behavior." I bump his hip. "You're a challenge to read."

Elaine beams at us when she sees me, then drinks in Lief. I know he's older than the majority of the crowd, especially considering he's friends with Gunner. But when he goes to get us some drinks, Elaine's jaw drops.

"He's so fucking sexy. How did you score that?"

"I have my ways." I shrug. But she keeps peppering me with questions until I sigh. "He's a friend of a friend. Introductions were made. Phone numbers exchanged."

She gives an appreciative whistle and I see a few other girls eying him like they'd be happy to do whatever it would take to get underneath him. When a stacked blonde flips her hair and strokes his chest, jealousy flairs, but Lief barely stops, he definitely doesn't say anything.

He gives me my drink, nods to Elaine and thanks her for the invitation, and takes a long drink.

Elaine mouths "wow" to me again, then flashes a huge grin. "You two have fun."

"I have a feeling I'm the oldest person here." Lief says softly.

"Possibly. I'd have to know how old you are to confirm." I step closer, so my hip is brushing his. Almost automatically, his hand strokes down my back, resting just above my ass. "How old are you?"

"Thirty-nine." No hesitation in his answer.

"You don't look a day over thirty-five." I compliment.

He shrugs.

We stand in silence, people watching for a bit. I start pointing people out and we talk about what they're doing, the odds they're going to get what they want and try to predict what they'll do. I finish my drink in record time, then turn, taking Lief's hand.

"Dance with me?"

"Didn't you say I should do the asking?"

"I did, but you haven't, and I want to feel you against me." I shrug.

Lief joins me on the dancefloor and cradles my hips with his. I wrap an arm around his neck as our bodies brush and grind to the beat. He wraps an arm around my belly, almost as if he's staking claim and I feel his nose brush my throat.

"Floral," He murmurs. "Sweet."

"Unlike me." I tease as I rub my ass against his lap.

A low rumble in his chest tells me he's laughing. That spark in his eyes and light smile ignite something hot and needy in my belly. His fingers tighten in my dress, and I feel something hard against my ass. Fuck *yes*.

"You're plenty sweet," He murmurs, lips against my ear.

Even that small brush of his mouth makes my knees weak.

I spin, then pull him close as I straddle his thigh, rubbing myself down on him. Lief locks his thick arm around my back so my tits brush his chest. His fingers stroke over my neck until I pull him down to continue our conversation.

"You don't know that for sure. You haven't had a taste of me yet, Viking," I purr.

I think I hear him groan, but I *know* I feel that hardness grow against my belly. Holy hell, he's big everywhere. He spins me and we continue dancing through the song. I find every possible excuse to touch him, stroke him, rub myself on him.

Another song leads to more teasing, especially considering his fingers trace the outside of my breast and down my side, sending shivers rippling across my skin, tightening my nipples into sensitive peaks that can barely handle the fabric of my dress.

Being so close to him is raising my temperature until I'm ready to strip myself and get some relief from the sweat dewing at my hairline.

But I lean back against Lief and try to pull his hand up to cup my breast, not giving a single shit who sees.

"I'd like a proper taste of you, Valerie." He says against my throat.

"Define proper." I encourage, steadily losing myself in his words, his body, the promises that are weaving with my own expectations. "So I know what I'm in for."

Rather than explain, he spins me until we're off the dance floor. I wave my hand at my face and Lief guides me through a door so we're in the bracing cold. I gasp and wrap my arms around myself only for Lief to pin me to the wall, his body working like a space heater to balance out the little flurry of snow.

"Why are we outside?" I ask.

"I don't want to be interrupted. Do you?"

"Depends on what you're planning." I reach up to tap his temple. "I never know what's going on in there."

Lief brushes his lips across my temple, his fingers stroking along my jaw, so light and gentle that I lean into his hand. "Think of our conversation, Valerie."

But all I can think of is his fingers moving across my throat, raising goosebumps as his other hand brushes my hip, gripping the fabric of my dress tightly. He raises my chin until I look up at him and he strokes the pad of his thumb over my bottom lip.

My mouth opens for him and I let out a shaky breath. Where's all my sass and sarcasm and quick comments? "You want … me?"

He nods, his nose brushing mine. "Apparently, I haven't been obvious enough."

"No." I agree, standing on my toes so there's only a millimeter between our mouths – maybe. "You should show me."

His breath rushes over my face and I try to jerk him closer to me. "Now. You should show me now."

He hesitates one more moment, then presses his mouth to mine. I braid my fingers into his hair, jerking him down tighter as I lick across his bottom lip. Lief groans cups the back of my neck and kisses me harder. His tongue flicks against mine before plunging deep into my mouth. He plunders me, claims me, makes my knees weak and my head light with his kiss.

All I can do is hold on and take what he gives. His hand slides to my ass, then he jerks me up and into his arms. My legs wrap around him obediently as he pins me to the wall, his cock pressing right where I need him.

Groaning, I rub myself against him, pull him tighter, lose myself in his mouth and his body as we make out in the cold. He feels so fucking good, tastes even better, and the sounds that leave his throat as I suck his tongue drive me insane.

We should have been doing this all night. Fuck dancing, fuck this party, I just want to fuck him. Right now, right here. He pulls back, looks at my face, then kisses me again, faster and harder, one hand on the wall behind me as he meets every thrust of my hips with one of his own. I whimper and my head falls back.

"Fuck, Lief." I pant.

His mouth continues down my throat, licking, kissing, then biting over the pulse point. I dig my nails into his shoulders and offer more of myself to him as my legs tighten, pulling him closer. He has to be able to feel how wet I am, even though his jeans.

Fuck, just the friction between him, the way he's kissing me, touching me, it's nearly enough to get me off. His lips take another tour of my throat before he bites my ear. Every panting breath catches the lingering dampness on my neck.

"I was right." He murmurs. "Sweet."

"We should go back to my place," I pant.

"What about the party?" He draws back, blinking a few times. "You don't want to stay?"

I roll my hips on his and he groans, pressing his forehead to mine. "Behave, Valerie."

"I can't do that when you're touching me." I knot my fingers in his shirt and jerk him back to my mouth. I nibble his bottom lip and kiss him again. "I don't want to. I want you on top of me in bed."

He considers it, heat and hunger in his eyes, but then his phone vibrates against my thigh. I shake my head. "No. Leave it. Please."

"I wish I could." He gives me another kiss while untangling himself from my legs and grabbing his phone.

I'm so not ready to be done. I want to at least blow him, at least give him incentive to stay. So I rub him through his jeans, my hands stroking his thick cock, fingers tightening around him. He grabs my hand and pins it above my head, his forehead pressing to mine as he answers the phone.

"Yes?"

I like that husky voice on him, the obvious desire in his eyes, the way he still hasn't let me go. But then he switches. From hot and eager, to focused, professional. Releasing me, he takes a step back, glancing down the road.

"Now?"

Shaking my head, I try to reclaim him. Sighing, he nods. "Very well."

He hangs up and pulls me close to give me another kiss. "I have to go."

"But, we … we were just … Lief!" I complain, my brain still struggling to pull out of the hot moment we shared.

"If I had a choice ..." His eyes stroke down over my body and he doesn't have to finish the sentence for me to understand. I groan, but let him haul me back to his car. "I am very sorry to cut our night short, Valerie."

"You and me both," I grumble.

CHASE

I finish checking Stefan's social media accounts, then stretch back in my chair. My back cracks in about three places as I lift my arms. A boring night, as most are. Dad doesn't understand all the potential and possibilities when it comes to hacking or tracking on the computer.

He's married to the old ways of doing things. Rolling out my neck, I check on a few other things, things I wasn't asked to check on, but I think are important. Plenty of people in our organization are online and have large footprints – via email, social media, or mentions in articles. I start putting together a few things, then see Hunter pop up.

The paparazzi caught us both leaving a club and luckily only cited us as millionaire bachelors that any woman would be lucky to have on her arm. As far as they know, we just have a huge inheritance and the family business is doing well. We're a way to spice up the news or press when Hollywood stars and political figures are behaving a little to well.

With Hunter, they never have a problem putting together enough to make a scandalous one-minute story. Making us both simple and reducing us to rumors apparently makes for a better story.

Just as I start looking at the comments, seeing how we're trending online and making sure the wrong things don't come up, my office door opens. Turning, I see Hunter, looking pissed and focused.

Never a good combination. "How can I help you, bro?"

He shuts and locks the door, glances around, then sits beside me. "As a warning, what I'm going to tell you will piss our father off and if you choose to do it, it has to be done perfectly."

"Thanks for being cryptic. If it's computer shit, you know I'll do it perfectly. No need for the threat."

"And you don't care about pissing off the old man, do you?" He chuckles. "Alright. I have Lief coming back as well, so we can approach this together."

"Why? If Dad gave it to you, aren't you supposed to handle it alone?"

"Fuck that." He scoffs. "I know you're willing to try new things when it comes to … business."

"And pleasure," I smirk.

He rolls his eyes. "Focus, please. This is important."

Hunter isn't usually so serious, even when it comes to assignments Dad gives him. It must be bad, or at minimum, a test from the old man. I nod to Hunter and motion for him to continue. He pulls out a manila envelope and shows me the paperwork.

"So? What about Mr. Smith?"

Hunter opens his mouth, but his phone rings. Pulling it to his ear, he nods. "Hey, Lief. Head to Chase's office. No distractions. No guests."

A moment later and Lief joins us, locking the door behind him. His face is colder than normal, eyes almost pissed. If I didn't know better, I'd say we interrupted something. Before I can give him shit, Hunter taps the folder.

Lief nods. "What's the verdict?"

"What's the fucking question!" I demand.

Hunter smooths his shirt. "A manila envelope means a choice – a hit or an interview. Mr. Smith got through one interview, but apparently, he hasn't earned the necessary trust."

I swallow that knowledge and try to move on right away. I can't focus on the inescapable proof that my dad orders things like that. Of course, a part of me knew, but knowing that it's a probability and then knowing it's an actual thing is … different.

"The verdict?" Lief demands, frustration obvious.

"I'm sorry, did I pull you from something important?" Hunter growls.

"Yes."

I blink at Lief. I figured he just read or something in his free time. Hunter arches an eyebrow and motions for Lief to share. He doesn't. I interrupt their pissing contest. "You said no distractions, Hunt. Why this meeting?"

"Because Lief *isn't* going to be involved in this and I wanted to make that clear. My plan is for you, Chase, to go through his computer and make sure there is no issue, that he can be trusted. Lief's methods, though successful, may raise questions that lead back to us in ways that would cause issues. If you can hack into his system and verify that he's clean, everyone is safe, the police stay out of it, and our job is done."

"You didn't need me here." Lief hisses. "That could have been stated over the phone."

72

"Considering I'm sure my father saw you walk in, he will be patient and allow Chase to do the job before trying to follow up with you on my decision."

Lief grumbles something in a language I don't know, then walks out, slamming the door behind him. Hunter shrugs, "whatever. Can you do this?"

"Yeah."

"Now?"

"Sure, who needs sleep." I roll my eyes.

"Not you if we want Mr. Smith alive. If this fails, if you miss something, we're both fucked. You understand the stakes?"

"You've made it inescapably clear, Hunt. Let's get on with it."

He nods, adjusts in his chair, and waits for me to do some magic with the computer. Hunter's smart, but he's not into computers and I know that. He'd rather read books on history, on physics, on everything he can possibly get his hands on … other than anything relating to coding.

"You're going to sit here and watch?" I confirm.

He nods, simple and direct. "Let's go."

I force myself to ignore him and follow the necessary chains to get to where I need to be. It takes time to hack into his system, but luckily Dad had the foresight to encourage me to establish backdoors into the systems of those we work with. He's paranoid, but in this case, I guess it's helpful.

As long as it proves Mr. Smith is innocent.

I get into the accounting information, make sure all of that is there, check his email, check his search history, and go through everything with a fine-tooth comb. It takes *hours*. Hunter brings me coffee and doesn't leave my side. In fact, he encourages me, asks questions about

73

certain things I'm checking, and asks if there is any way that we can also check his phone.

"I'd need to actually look at his phone to check anything there, but if he uses the same email to connect them, then the search history should line up to a degree. I'm not seeing anything that would link him to any leak of information."

Hunter takes a slow breath, studying the screen as if something would jump out. "You checked deleted things?"

"Yes. I checked the trash folders, the logs, anything not deleted from the hard drive. I don't think he has a motive either. We pay him well, really well. How could he benefit by going to the police?"

"Logic goes out the window when morals are involved."

Hunter relaxes back into his seat. "If you consider him clear, I'm going to say he's good and report this accordingly, including your involvement. Prepare for some trouble in the next few days, but I'll wait until after we meet with Stefan to say anything to father."

"Okay." I shrug. "Or you could let me do it. I don't give a shit if the man likes me."

Hunter shakes his head. "This is my job. Get some sleep."

"You should probably check on Lief," I murmur while getting out of Mr. Smith's computer. "It takes a lot to piss him off and you did a royally good job of that."

Hunter tells me not to worry about it and I head to bed. I should be exhausted, but instead, my mind is on Valerie. If this shit with Stefan doesn't work, she's going to get dragged into all this. We'll have to protect her and our reputations, and hide our secrets.

Which is a losing battle. But … but I'd love to see her all the same. It's nearly eight in the morning, so I send her a text, reminding her she has an invitation to a date night with me. I roll over, not expecting an answer.

When I get up around two in the afternoon, I see a response.

VALERIE: Maybe next weekend. I'm busy all week with work.

A maybe is better than no. And a time frame.

CHASE: Don't be a stranger until then. I like your messages.

VALERIE: You like a whole lot more than my messages.

I smirk, then chuckle. She's not wrong about that. Valerie has plenty of assets. Her hot body, that sass, how quick witted she is, she's fucking fearless, and damn does she leave fantastic memories.

CHASE: All the more reason to take you out next weekend. You know how much I like to please.

VALERIE: Keep sweetening the pot and I won't have a way to say no.

CHASE: You need more tempting?

She doesn't answer, so I shrug and pocket my phone. I have plenty to do today to keep me busy. Like inviting Stefan to the strip club – which he happily accepts as long as I pay, then let Hunter know that it's set, and getting ready for the meeting.

I notice Lief is M.I.A. but Hunter's not concerned. He paces across the floor. "I feel like we need some kind of upper hand when it comes to Stefan. I've tried studying some psychology shit, but I think we should give our friend a call."

"We agreed-"

"Just a phone call, Chase. I don't need her showing up to the strip club in disguise trying to fish for information while getting dollars tucked into her thong." But his eyes darken at the idea and I'm sure he'd love for Valerie to give him a private dance.

"Just a phone call."

"And Lief?"

"Has earned himself some personal time," Hunter grumbles. He dials his phone and when the ringing stops, he gives a wolfish smile. "Still answering for me, sweetheart?"

"What do you want?" Valerie grumbles.

"Advice."

"Look, if you need help figuring out how to charm a woman, there are plenty of resources online." She teases.

"Awe, we both know I've taken care of that with you or you wouldn't be so sweet to me." He flirts until I arch an eyebrow. "You're on speaker by the way. Me and Chase."

"Hi, Chase. Also, no to your earlier question."

It's my turn to smile.

My brother rolls his eyes. "We need to know how to get information from someone without them really knowing they're giving information."

"Depends on the personality."

"Narcissistic, entitled, dick-ish." Hunter says. "And before you accuse me, it's someone else."

"Get the person talking about themselves. People like to share and it makes them like you more. Alcohol loosens tongues, so do distractions. Ask for a small favor, maybe pretend you have an issue related to the stuff you want to know and see if he'll give you advice. I could give you a whole list."

"Please do."

"But personality is important here. If something doesn't work, don't keep pushing. I'm serious. It can backfire fast. Try those basics. They work more often than not. Good luck."

"Thank you, sweetheart. I'll pay you back with a nice dinner and more soon."

"Or you can try that conversation tactic, I mentioned before," She says. "Bye."

With that, she's gone. Hunter nods to me, not put off at all by Valerie's dismissal. "We have the tools, let's make this shit work and earn ourselves some free time."

"You actually want to pursue Valerie when you know I like her?"

"I could ask you the same." He shrugs. "But I did happen to bring up giving her what her bestie has and she's mentioned it a few times."

I think that over as I get ready for the club. Sharing Valerie with my brother and Lief, all of us enjoying her, touching her, fucking her … Hunter has certainly had worse ideas.

VALERIE

The intercom by my door buzzes after I hang up with Hunter. At least he turned down his flirting in front of his brother. And Chase is tempting as hell. If it's possible at all, I'll be on that cruise with him this weekend.

"Hello?" I ask after pressing the button.

"We have unfinished business, Valerie." Lief's husky voice teases me even over the crackling speaker.

I shiver and pinch myself to make sure this is real. Yup. Pinching hurts. Lief is downstairs. I buzz him up instead of bothering with teasing. I unlock my door open it, and by the time I step out, I see him stalking down the hallway toward me.

Putting a hand on my hip, I arch an eyebrow. "You didn't even kiss me goodbye when you dropped me off here yesterday."

"I wouldn't have left." He says before tipping my chin up and kissing me hard.

So much for resisting him. I melt against his mouth, clutching his shirt as he picks me up, wraps me around him, and walks me into my apartment.

He shuts the door behind him and continues kissing me, feasting on my mouth, licking and nipping across my jaw, then biting my throat again.

"Oh." I moan, eyes fluttering shut

"You have many post-it notes."

I look around and nod. "I forget things easily."

He drops me on my bed and looks me over. "Pants."

"Useless inside." I don't care that I only have on a tank top and panties. It's not like I was planning for company. And it's not like Lief is complaining. I stretch on my bed, flashing more skin as I look Lief over. "So, unfinished business?"

"Yes." But he just keeps watching. "If you're still interested."

"I think you need to use those words you know to tell me what I'm in for." As if I don't know exactly what he wants, exactly what he has planned.

"I've made you wait twice now." He gets on his knees on the bed, angling himself over me. "I'm not going to draw it out any more."

I put my foot on his chest, holding him in place. "My house my rules. Use your words."

"I'm going to make you come." He strokes up my leg. "With my fingers." He kisses the inside of my knee. "My mouth." His hands catch on my panties. "And my cock."

Is that me shaking or him?

"Now?" My voice is a squeak.

"Now." He agrees, dragging me toward him by my hips and pushing my legs apart. Before I can think to push him away, he holds my wrists above my head, locked in just one of his big hands. His other slowly guides my shirt up, stopping just under my breasts. "If your answer is yes."

79

"Fuck yes," I pant.

Lief groans and kisses me hard and deep, making sure I know exactly how much he wants me. He grinds against me, his cock hard as a rock already. I squirm against his hold on me, wanting to touch him, to strip him, to get on top of him right fucking now.

"Patience." He purrs against my lips.

But then he pulls my shirt up to my chin and licks across the top curve of my breast before kissing between them. "Beautiful."

"Lief!" My back arches. "Please!"

But he takes his fucking time, kissing slowly, teasing me with his finger circling closer and closer to my nipple until he finally rolls it between his fingers while sucking and licking my other. I squirm against him, tugging on my wrist despite his firm grasp, needing more than the gentle flick of his tongue and his soft touches.

"I'm not going to fucking break," I growl.

His eyes flick to me, deadly dangerous. He pinches my nipple, punishing me for my comment. But it's not a fucking punishment, it's a reward. I moan and my head falls back. Lief echoes the sound against my skin.

His hand strokes down my belly, then he's dragging my underwear down my thighs. I shift to help, impatient, wet, and needy as hell. I want him inside me *now*. Before we can be interrupted again by anything or anyone

But his fingers tease my slit, even while my ankles are tangled in my panties. My hips rock against his hand and he lightly bites my breast. Gasping, I try to spread my legs, clumsy and demanding.

Two of his fingers circle my clit, stroke down to my entrance, dip in as a tease, then back to my clit, rubbing hard and fast. I moan and ride his fingers, increasing the pressure just like I need.

"Fuck." I moan.

"So wet, Valerie."

"Your fault." I pant. "Fuck, don't stop."

When I rock forward again, his fingers slip into me, filling me so much better than my own. They're so much bigger than mine, so much better. My eyes flutter shut as sparks catch across my body. His teeth digging into my throat, his fingers thrusting in and out of my wet pussy again and again as his thumb rubs my clit.

Oh, it's too much. My back arches and I let out a hoarse yell as I come for him, pleasure ripping through my body until I'm a shaking mess. Lief kisses me before I can catch my bearings and makes me come for his fingers again. And again.

He releases my hands, but they stay put. I'm dizzy, my eyes are heavy, and all I can do is tell him how good he feels. I feel something against my lips and open my mouth obediently. Lief's fingers push into my mouth, stroking along my tongue so I can taste myself there. Groaning, I suck his fingers, then lick between them.

He jerks his hand back and my eyes open just for him to kiss me, his tongue teasing mine as I give in and tug on his shirt, pulling it off him and continuing to kiss him as my body rolls against him.

Lief's skin is hot, soft, and silky. I stroke over his chest and abs until I tug on his belt. He grabs my hands and chuckles. "So impatient."

"I want you," I complain.

"Be good and you get to have everything you want." He promises before kissing me again. "Spread your legs for me."

I do as I'm told, holding them up and apart as Lief sits up on his knees. He looks me over and licks across his bottom lip. My legs are shaking from that searing gaze alone. He jerks me closer and nearly bends me in half so he can devour my pussy as I watch.

Whimpering, I try to move against his tongue, try to get him right where I need him, but one of his arms locks around my middle, holding me against him, almost upside down as he licks deeper and flattens his tongue over my clit.

"Oh fuck." I moan.

Lief's breath rushes over my pussy, making my legs twitch as he continues the maddening pace. No fantasy comes close to him or his sinful tongue. Groaning, I give up the fight and surrender control. He sucks and laps at my clit until my body tightens and I grip the sheets, trying to hold on and hold out.

It's useless. I give in with his name on my tongue as I shatter all over again. But he doesn't stop, he only adds his fingers, plunging even deeper into me at this angle. I don't get the chance to come down from orgasm one, I just tumble into the second one, feeling the rumble of his satisfaction as I do.

When he releases me and gets up, I just flop to the bed. I roll onto my side, trying to catch my breath, trying to get my pussy to stop quivering as pleasure threatens to consume me all over again.

"Fucking hell, Lief." I pant. "You've been holding out on me."

He shucks his pants. "And you're better than I fantasized."

"You were fantasizing about me?" I hum, eying his very hard, very big cock. "While touching yourself?"

His hand strokes over his length. "Of course, Valerie. I thought my interest was obvious."

"Nothing about you is obvious." I crawl across the bed and lick the head of his cock.

Lief takes a step forward and bundles my hair up in one of his hands. "You want to blow me?"

"Yes," I groan.

He nods and I stretch my lips to fit around him. My tongue swirls around the tip, then I sink deeper, as deep as I can go. He groans and his abs tighten as I bob up and down. God, he's so thick, so good, perfect.

I grab his taught ass to drive myself further down his cock, nearly gagging as I try to get to the base. Lief's hand guides me off him, then he tosses me back on the bed easily.

Holy fuck, the tattoos, the huge expanse of muscle that covers him, that starving, wild look in his eyes, all of it is pure sex. Lief follows me as I back up until my head hits my pillow. He slides his fingers into my hand to hold me down, then kisses me hungrily.

"You have no idea what you do to me," He growls. "How good you taste." Another kiss. "How good you feel."

"I like you talkative." I breathe.

He shoves his tongue between my lips and thrusts into me hard. My back arches and I cling to him as he stretches my pussy around his cock. I grind against him until his arm comes down over my hips. He presses ever so slightly, then thrusts into me again.

Fuck, I feel him everywhere. The sprinkling of hair across his chest, teases my nipples, his thighs under my slick legs, his mouth making a map of hickeys and bite marks across my neck and shoulder.

"Yes," I moan.

He picks up the pace, driving into me like he needs to fuck me to live. His hands stroke over my arms, down my sides, touching wherever he can until he grabs my ankles and pushes my legs toward my ears.

God, he's so fucking deep inside me. "Lief, yes. Oh fuck, just like that."

He kisses my calf, then presses down on me harder, owning me with every roll of his hips, claiming me as his over and over again until his name is the only word in my head. My eyes flutter shut and moans rip through me. Ecstasy itself waves through me again and again, coming faster and faster until it's impossible for me to resist him, to think, to do anything but give in.

"Lief!" I scream his name and drag my nails down his arms.

I'm pretty sure I black out with the force of the orgasm. My vision is hazy, everything is warm and comfortable. Then I feel his hands rolling me over. I open my eyes sleepily and realize I'm on my knees and elbows.

Looking back over my shoulder, I find Lief, face flushed, jaw tight, as he rubs himself against me. "More?"

"Don't stop until you come," I order.

He grins, a full and complete smile then slams into me. I bounce on his cock, giving as much as he does, even as my legs shake and slip across the sheets. He holds my hip in one hand and grips my hair tightly in the other so I can't smother a single moan.

This time when I come, faster than I'd hoped since I'm seriously fucking enjoying this, I see stars. Lief lets out a wild growl, bites the back of my shoulder, and shudders as he finishes with me. I laugh as we collapse and rub across his thigh.

"Holy fucking hell," I moan.

"Give me a little and we can go again," He promises, kissing the bite mark I know I have on my back.

There has to be some kind of god if Lief can really give me this all over *again* tonight.

LIEF

J clean up after Valerie, then come into her room, to see her reading a book. She's wearing my shirt, not even buttoned, laying on her belly as she turns the page. Her legs all exposed, the bottom curve of her ass teasing me.

I wrap my hand around her ankle and drag her down the bed, making her squeal as she giggles and tries to roll over. I climb on top of her and kiss her neck. She moans and I feel her press against me, even through the towel.

"Sexy Viking man," She says as I nibble across her shoulder.

She is sweet, even if she doesn't want to believe it. The way she responds immediately and gives in with just the right touch.

"What are you reading?" I ask against her skin.

"A book on prolonged exposure therapy. It can wait."

"Willing to put work aside?"

"Fun reading," She corrects, rolling under me. "Not as much fun as you."

What a compliment. I kiss her passionately, cupping the back of her head in my hand. She's not half as controlled. She tugs on my towel and rubs her hand over my cock. It hardens just from that teasing brush of her fingers and palm.

"More?"

"Impatient," I say against her lips.

"You're in high demand," She corrects, pushing me back to climb on top of me. "I'm not wasting time while I have you. Unless you're suddenly talkative outside of sex."

"What do you want to know?" I ask.

"Just ... everything."

Everything is too big. I keep watching her as she rubs herself against me.

"You said you're from Europe. Where?"

"We traveled often," I murmur, grabbing her hips to stop her teasing. "I was born in Ireland and grew up in the Netherlands, Norway, and Denmark. I came to the U.S. for college. It was ... a very intense change."

"Which was your favorite?"

"Denmark," I answer immediately. "Perhaps you'd like it."

"I've never left the country." She muses, tracing a tattoo across my chest. A Viking ship on fire. "I don't even have a passport."

"You should fix that," I say gently. "Everyone should have one."

"Tell me something I don't know about you, Viking.." She presses her lips to my neck. "Something interesting."

"I have no internal dialogue." I run my fingers through her hair, then press a kiss near her ear. "My thoughts just ... connect. There's no back and forth."

"No wonder you said you're simple," She says against my collarbone. "That only raises about a million more questions. You know that right?"

I put her on her back and grind against her, watching her eyes flutter. "Look it up or save them for later."

"Round two?" She asks.

I kiss her eagerly as an answer. My tongue drags across her lips until she opens for me, but she nips at my tongue. I groan and bite her hard. She shivers and drags her nails down my back.

Rough little hellcat.

"I'm going to fuck you until you can't take anymore, pet," I warn.

"Good," She pants. "I want all of you that I can get. Right here. Right now."

It's a challenge. I fuck her again on the bed, memorizing every soft sound she makes. But when she tries to go clean up, I shove her against the wall, rub myself against her from behind and kiss down her back, following her spine.

She shivers. "Lief."

I bite her ass and she whimpers, the muscle tightening under her skin before she pushes back against my mouth as I kiss the spot. I smack her ass. "Spread your legs."

"Make me." She teases, wiggling her butt at me.

I bite her upper thigh, growling as I dig my teeth in. She moans and hits the wall before I let up. I force her legs apart, jerk her hips back and devour her pussy again. Lapping at her clit, claiming her the only way I can.

She rides my mouth, doesn't hide a single sound, then comes for me again. Standing up, I push two fingers into her wetness. Her head falls

back and she reaches back to stroke my cock. "Fuck, you're going to
…"

A moan cuts her off and I thrust my fingers into her harder before
moving them forward and back, hitting all those sensitive spots that
she needs to be touched. Valerie trembles and whimpers before
coming again.

"I like how you come, viper," I whisper in her ear. "Especially when I
know it's for me."

"You're so good," She murmurs, wavering on her feet.

"We're just getting started."

I prove it by making her get on her knees. She licks and sucks,
showing me again what her mouth can do. I keep my hand in her hair
as she brings me closer and closer to the edge. Pleasure teases my
head, threatening to drag me down, but I'm not ready to come.

I jerk away from her and she whimpers. "I didn't finish!"

Scooping her up, I toss her in bed. She gasps as she hits the mattress. I
sit on the bed and look her over, ready to ravage her. I pat my lap and
she comes immediately, straddling me and sliding herself down over
every inch.

I groan and drag my nails down her back, watching her groan as she
braces herself on my shoulders. She tests me with a few rolls of her
body, then bounces on me, her tits moving with her until I cup one
and bend over to suck her nipple.

Her nails scrape across my skin as she tries not to fall. All she can do is
grind on me and she does, moving against me until I feel her pussy
quiver. She's on the edge. That's my cue. I thrust into her hard, dragging her back with me, squeezing her to my chest as I ram into her
again and again.

All she can do is take it.

"Lief! Lief!" She howls my name as she comes again.

I pull out, giving myself two seconds to stop my orgasm, before putting her on her feet and bending her over the bed. She hums something in her throat, but then I'm inside her again, holding her hands in place as I lick and kiss her throat while fucking her.

When she wiggles against me, then adds to every thrust by bouncing against me, I know I'm fucked. I can't hold out, not with her. Not forever. We come apart together and I quiet my groan by digging my teeth into her shoulder.

She loses her footing and falls to the bed, panting and struggling to catch her breath. I smile as I take care of myself, then I pull her into bed, trying to get her comfortable. She jerks me in with her and fits herself to my side.

I'm not a cuddler, not really. But she feels good. Warm, soft, better than any pillow I've ever had.

"Just hold me for a few minutes." She asks, voice hoarse and dry. "I like cuddling."

When I don't move my arms, Valerie grabs my hand and pulls it around her hip. I clutch her ass and she giggles, moving closer and nuzzling my neck. It's too sweet, too intimate. I clear my throat, but she squeezes me tighter and tangles our legs.

I raise my other hand to stroke through her hair and the sound that she gives me is so satisfied and warm that I do it again while kissing her forehead.

"I used to dream about going to Europe." She says softly. "About actually going on adventures instead of watching other people get to have them on T.V."

"What kind?" I ask.

"So many different kinds." She tugs on a strand of my hair before stroking across my chest. "The normal tourist kind of adventure where I just go find peace and fun. The Indiana Jones kind where there's action and treasure. The kind where I end up helping a spy or have to get out of some intense issue where life is on the line. Where I get magical powers for no reason."

I chuckle and feel her lips press above my racing heart. "My life isn't that exciting, Viking. But when I watch a movie or read a book, I get to experience something totally different … until the last page or the credits. Then it's over and … and I'm still in my little apartment alone with school and work waiting."

"Normal can be nice," I comment softly. "All that action …"

She lifts her head to look at me. "What, Lief?"

"Don't you think it would get to be too much after a while? That your morals would start to leave? Everything is about survival … it's exciting until it's exhausting."

She considers that, actually thinks about my words before shrugging. "I guess the grass is always greener. You do crazy security work and I take care of people."

I trace her puffy bottom lip. "I like how you take care of me."

"Sex isn't taking care of someone." She rolls her eyes, then slowly rolls me fully onto my back to kiss across my chest with slow, excruciating patience. "And *this* is aftercare."

"What's your definition then?"

"Taking care of someone is prioritizing their health, making them …" Her breath brushes across my skin. "Making them feel like they matter, like every little detail is vitally important, caring about their wellness, their life, their feelings."

I stroke over her cheek and feel her lean into my hand. Her eyes shut and she doesn't complain when I just take the time to study her face. So calm, so relaxed, soft, and approachable when she isn't in public.

Valerie is different from anyone I've ever met. I lean forward and hesitate, my nose brushing hers. She takes a shuddering breath. "Lief, you make patience feel like torture."

I kiss her softly, then slowly kiss her again. Our lips mold together and my hand slides back into her hair as I tighten my hold on her. She feels good, right, like she should be mine and mine alone.

I draw back before she can take control, then roll her over, pressing her into the bed as her toes rub across my ankle. My lips hover over hers as my hair brushes her cheek. This woman is more dangerous than any order or hitman.

She whimpers under me, but her fingers stay soft as she strokes over my body. My hips roll, a reaction I can't control. She bites her bottom lip and arches her back, lifting to try and kiss me.

I keep that millimeter of space between us. My lips part. "You make being taken care of sound ... pleasant."

"It can be." Her fingers tease my throat, then she presses her palm to my pulse. "Do you want me to take care of you Lief?"

My heart lurches uncomfortably in my chest. I take a ragged breath. She's offering more than she knows. I could say yes. But that word is stuck.

"You're big and strong." She whispers, lips pressing to my jaw. "I'm sure people think you don't need anything soft, that you don't need anything at all. And I know Hunter and Chase well enough to know they don't think about things like that."

"You do," I murmur.

She nods but feels how hard I am against her hip. She adjusts the position so I'm pressed against her pussy. I could slide right in. She's still wet. Her hand pushes my hair back, but I can't look away from her warm eyes, as welcoming as a fire in *real* winter.

She's a threat. My body disagrees, but I *know* it.

Valerie brushes her lips over mine. "Are you going to fuck me again, Viking?"

"No." I murmur, despite kissing her again, my tongue slowly brushing hers. "I'm going to take care of you."

VALERIE

*L*ief taking care of me involves the shower. He keeps a hand on me as he turns it on as if I'm going to run. Which is fucking impossible considering how sexy he is … and the fact that my legs are barely more than jelly.

"I like showers as hot as they can be," He murmurs.

"Good," I agree.

He guides me in with him, then orders me to stand in one spot. I have to support myself against the wall. He looks me over slowly and his cock taps his belly again. It's distracting me like crazy. "We should do something about that."

"No." He catches my hand before I can touch him and holds it against the wall of the shower.

I bite my bottom lip as his grip tightens on me and his eyes sharpen. I shiver and revel in the fact that he has total control. Lief presses his body against mine. This level of dominance is so … so hot. The blatant hunger and desire being pushed down, his control, all of it is so maddening, so overwhelming.

"But-" I start.

The tip of his nose brushes along my jaw and I turn my head, ready for him to kiss my neck, to bite me, to do anything and everything he wants to me. But instead, my loofah scrubs along my hip or up my side. I whimper at the sudden change.

"I'm taking care of you," He insists. "Let me."

And I do. He teases my body with the loofah, rubbing over every bit of my body. And I'm not allowed to clean his. He does that himself, only letting me watch. I ache for him, burn for him, but if he can manage this much control to be soft with me ...I want to take advantage of it.

"Lief," I beg.

But he steps out of the shower and holds up a fresh towel for me. I step into it and feel him tighten it around me before he nudges my legs apart and uses the towel to rub between my legs. I shiver and bite my lip.

"You're killing me."

He stands up, cups his hand around the back of my neck and holds me just far enough away that I can't kiss him, but I can feel his breath. "When I leave, I want you still thinking of me."

"It's impossible not to think of you." Honesty comes easily.

But I'm not allowed to kiss him, to touch him, nothing until he's dressed. Then he jerks me against him and gives me a kiss that my *soul* feels. Crushing me against his mouth and taking everything. All I can do is react, moan, try to beg for more with my tongue and hope it doesn't end.

Lief threads his fingers through my hair and pulls me back to bite my bottom lip. "I want you to be able to remember me without a sticky-note."

"I will." I cling to him. "One more time?"

He considers it, then his lips turn up. "Moderation, Valerie."

And with that, he's out the door, leaving me a panting, breathless mess. We fucked three times and I still want more. I want his hands on me, I want more satisfaction. I groan as I fall back in bed, then jump up to lock the door to find he already took care of that.

I take a picture of myself with the towel open, only covering my pussy, and send it to Lief.

The response is immediate.

LIEF: Next time.

I groan and bury my face in my pillow. But when I turn the lights out, planning on going a solo session, but I'm too comfortable, too tired, too … pleased. I fall right asleep. When I get up, I scramble to grab my things when I see the time, only to notice it's Sunday.

Sighing, I drop back in bed. Turning, I stretch in bed before smiling. Lief didn't need to be worried about me forgetting him. How could I possibly forget that toe curling night? From wild beginning to frustrating end, every detail is etched into my head. The sounds he made as he was inside me, the way he gave me his entire, unflinching attention all night, and every bit of pleasure he gave.

He spoiled me right up to the end. And then that no to another round, him not letting me do the taking care of … Who knew being denied could be so hot?

I take the day to focus on myself and take care of things at home, drinking so much water I'm sloshy, making myself a full meal to satisfy my growling belly, and cleaning, even though I want to leave my pillow cases because they smell like Lief. It feels silly, but when I press a pillow to my face and smell that mix of spice and earthy tones, I moan and give in.

Collapsing in bed, I check my phone. Elaine asks me how my night ended Friday with a winky face and I laugh and send her a zipper faced emoji. I'm not sharing a damn thing about Lief.

But the text from Chase is a little more demanding.

CHASE: I can't stop thinking about how you taste.

My legs tighten painfully and I whimper

VALERIE: Are you free this weekend? You'll have more than a taste.

We leave it at that and then I check the news, preparing for any new clients. Lo and behold, the bane of my existence and his brother are on the front page. I snort to myself and pull my blanket tighter around me.

"Millionaire playboys were seen leaving a strip club with smiles on their faces and no ones in their pockets." I roll my eyes.

It's not fair, I know. I shouldn't expect Chase or Hunter to only get their kicks with me, but still. A strip club? Really? After asking me how to help get information out of a friend? But I see another picture of them with a guy who isn't Lief.

Of course, it's not Lief. Lief was here for ninety percent of the night showing me exactly how much like heaven torture can feel. I do a reverse image search on the guy and find his name.

Stefano Rossi. Rossi … that name feels familiar, but the article fills me in. Heir to an empire of money, rumors, and old time – obviously cut – mafia life. I rub my thumb over my bottom lip, then bite the nail without breaking it.

"Why would Hunter want information from you?" I murmur.

My phone rings, making me jump and I rub my eyes before I answer it on speaker. "Hello?"

"Saturday?" Chase asks.

Now that I know their last name – Volkov, I do a search. They're everywhere. Paparazzi eat them up. Every event, every outing, they're playboys, bouncing between women, flaunting their wealth.

"After that date, you suggested … maybe."

"Maybe?" He chuckles. "What got me downgraded?"

"My research."

A long pause answers me. "What research?"

"You and your brother are very familiar with the paparazzi," I murmur, playing with a sticky note. "I don't want to be in the public eye. Are reporters going to see us getting on the dinner cruise together? Are people going to be taking our pictures? Digging into my life?"

"No," He assures me. "No, Valerie. I don't want to put you through that."

"How was the strip club?"

He sighs. "Not very much fun while working. Thank you for those hints. They worked wonders."

I groan and pick up the sticky note telling me to keep my weekend clear. "What am I going to do with you, Chase?"

"What?"

"You're great in bed, but you're a closed book. Everything I know about you, I've learned in a google search."

"I think that's what dating is for."

I nibble my bottom lip. "You shared me with Hunter."

"And I'm sure Lief didn't leave hickies on himself." He chuckles.

I groan. "What are we doing?"

97

"Having fun. Tell me where to pick you up on Saturday and I'll be there."

"For the dinner cruise."

"Sure."

I narrow my eyes, sure that he's hiding something, but I'm not sure I care what it is. "Fine. If I survive the week and have energy to spare, you can have me."

"You'll survive."

I hang up without a goodbye. On Monday, I power through classes like crazy, until I'm sitting in my office. It's Zen as fuck. Or at least as Zen as I could make it. Books on the shelves along with plants and little sand gardens.

I get through my three patients, then look at my schedule for the week. It's basic, as I expected. I see Diana on the list for a video session on Wednesday and smile. She'll take up a solid hour, but I'm sure she'll share plenty of juicy details.

When I adjust in my seat, I think of being on something much better than a chair. My body floods with heat as I think of Lief on me, under me, inside me. Or being in the same positions with Chase. I squeeze my thighs, moan softly, then shake my head. No. No. This is a professional environment. I have to be professional. My thoughts, my actions, all of it.

But when I get home, I do a whole photo shoot, wearing lingerie that I haven't worn since I got it. I laugh and drink wine as I dance and pose. I get a call from Lief after sending him a photo. He's faster on the draw than his friends.

"Valerie, your teasing is …"

"Torture?" I ask before taking another drink. "What are you going to do about it?"

"If I didn't have work …"

"If I didn't have to study …" I bite my lip. "Maybe you can send me something back before you're all busy."

"How are you?"

"Good."

"Aren't you against one word answers?"

I play with my hair and say, "It's been a boring week compared to our night."

"It was a very good night." He says softly. "Aren't you taking care of yourself when I'm not there?"

"Is that your way of saying you don't want to take care of me after last time?" I ask with a tease

"I'm tempted to drive there," He growls. "And do it properly."

"One day, you have to let me take care of you. You know that right?" I purr. "Give and take with me."

"What if I just want to give?" He asks.

"Too bad."

He lets out a soft groan and I close my eyes and smile. "Soon, Viking. I'm not patient."

"I know," He assures me. "Soon."

Wednesday, I get a video from Hunter. He's stroking his cock through his boxers, his hand spreading around his girth while all I can do is watch. It's a tease, a wicked one that gets under my skin even when I want to hate the playboy.

HUNTER: You have to earn my cock, sweetheart. You know-how.

I send another photo, me sucking my fingers, my cheeks hollowed, eyes on the camera.

HUNTER: Close. Beg.

I grin.

VALERIE: You'll be the one begging for my mouth around your cock and even one taste of my pussy.

HUNTER: We'll see.

He sends another video, this one has sound, him moaning as he rubs himself through his boxers, rough and sure with each stroke. My mouth waters as I watch, totally entranced. His package is ... holy hell.

I whimper and rub my throat, right where he gripped me, thinking about that hunger in his eyes, the way a part of me ached to obey, to give in, to finally have everything he's offered. Then he grunts and lets out a panting laugh.

"It's yours when you want it, Valerie. All you have to do is be my good girl."

A shiver snakes down my spine as heat pools in my belly. Fuck, his sex voice is an instant aphrodisiac. I groan and slide my hand between my legs. I nearly lost my mind when these brothers were playing with me. I went completely insane with Lief. How the hell am I going to be able handle all of them, even if I have them one at a time?

Especially when I want them all at once.

HUNTER

*W*hen my little minx doesn't answer, I call her. The phone picks up and I smile when I hear her breathy hello.

"You sound turned on, sweetheart," I say while rolling my boxers down. "Are you going to do something about that?"

"Maybe." I can hear the trembling in her voice.

"Maybe doesn't sound very satisfying. What are you wearing?"

She swallows and I know that she's fighting herself. I grin. "My boxers are around my knees and you know that was all I had on."

"A t-shirt and leggings," She grumbles. "If you think-"

"I know you're going to be good for me because you want to be," I cut her off, my voice sharpening. "Because if you didn't want to play, you wouldn't have answered."

Silence answers me.

"Now, go lay down in bed for me and let me tell you just what to do."

"Make me," She bites out.

"If I was there, do you know what I'd do?"

"Fuck off?"

"I'd push you against the wall with my hand wrapped around your throat and kiss across your jaw. I'd get all the way to the corner of your mouth. Then I'd wrap your leg around my hip and let you feel just what you do to me."

She sucks in a hard breath.

"I'd grind against you until you whimper, but I still wouldn't kiss you." I soften my hand over my cock, prolonging it. "I'd tighten my hand on your throat to remind you who's in control, then tear your leggings right down your gorgeous legs and rub you through your panties."

"Hunter, I … I …" She keeps trailing off.

"Are you in bed?" I ask.

"Yes."

"Take off your leggings and touch yourself, nice and slow. If you misbehave, the phone call is over."

"I have a vibrator you asshole. I don't need you to get off." She hisses.

"By all means, don't let me stop you."

She doesn't hang up and I tighten my hand around my cock, groaning. "Good girl. Let me hear you play with your clit."

She pants then whimpers softly. I keep going, loving the game, loving her submission, no matter how she fights herself.

My head falls back and I close my eyes. "I'd get you all the way to edge without ever pushing a finger into you. Then, right when I stop, I'd kiss you before you could argue."

He breath hitches and she moans softly.

"How wet are you, sweetheart?"

"Wouldn't you like to know?"

"Take off your underwear and your shirt. I want you naked. Now," I order.

I hear rustling and feel my temper cool. She pushes every button every time. Making me ride the line between pissed off and pleased. I exhale and then hear her again.

"I didn't tell you to touch yourself."

"Too bad." She lets out a wicked moan and I can hear how wet she is as she works her fingers in. "I like how my fingers feel inside me. How my thumb rubs my clit. How I don't have to beg to get off."

"Valerie."

"Don't you want to hear me come again?" She asks before another moan tears through her. She pants. "Don't you want to know how hot and wet I am? How good I taste?"

Her moan is muffled and I can hear her sucking. I stroke my cock fast and hard, squeezing tight and imagining her mouth around me instead, sucking and licking, all her sass gone as I fill her throat.

"Thin line," I warn.

She moans. "I taste good, Hunter. My pussy must be the only sweet thing about me."

"I think you'd rather have me fucking your throat, filling that sassy mouth of yours with every inch while you gag and whimper thinking about how much I could please you," I growl

She gets louder, but I know it's not fake. I've learned the difference.

"I'm so much bigger than your fingers so get your fucking toy and work it into your pussy."

Silence answers, then she swallows. "Okay."

103

"Do not turn it on," I order. "You're going to slide it in slowly, as deep as you can, then all the way out. I don't care how good it feels, you're going to move that slow until I tell you otherwise."

"How do you know what I'm doing?" She huffs, despite how shaky she is. "I could be fucking myself hard and fast."

"But you're not, because you want this as much as I do." I've never been more sure in my life. "You like being chased, but you want satisfaction. You want me to throw you over my shoulder, rip your clothes off your body with my teeth and take control."

She whimpers and I picture her fucking herself. This should have been a video call. When she doesn't argue, I continue. "Faster."

Her moans increase, and her panting is high pitched, eager.

God, just hearing her is driving me insane. I shiver and thrust into my hand as I tighten it again. She sounds so good, so fucking perfect and I know that being inside her would be better. I wouldn't have a hope at controlling myself, not once she submits.

"Good girl," I praise. "Pinch your nipple, roll it between your fingers."

She takes a deep breath, then whimpers.

"Make yourself come. And don't you *dare* hide your face in a pillow." I order between gritted teeth.

"Fuck you," She pants.

"I know you want to. And when you behave, you'll get to," I tease her.

It doesn't take her long to come apart, shouting and whimpering as she comes apart. I come for her, back arched, jaw tight, groaning low and deep as heat and pleasure fires off every nerve in my body.

My muscles quiver and my abs tighten again as my hips thrust forward uselessly. I slump in the chair and smile. "See what happens when you're good?"

"I did it myself," She argues.

"Sure you did. I just made it better." I sigh. "Now, get to studying. That degree won't earn itself."

I hang up, clean up, and exhale slowly. Once I put myself together after hands down the best phone sex I've had, I head out of the house only to be stopped by my father. He motions me to a room and I see Lief and Chase already waiting for me.

The door shuts behind me with a thundering sound that echoes in my bones. Just like that, I'm wound tight again. Masturbating isn't good enough to keep me calm around my father.

I sit and fold my hands. Chase isn't afraid, he's furious – because he doesn't know what our father is capable of. I gave him a hint, but the man isn't afraid to get his hands dirty despite keeping Lief on a leash, chained and obedient.

"You said this was handled," Father growls. "You assured me that you took care of it."

"I did."

"Mr. Smith hasn't been brought in and I know he's still alive. Explain to me then, how did you take care of the leak?"

"He's *not* the leak," I say as I cross my ankle over my knee.

"Proof."

"Chase." I look to my brother.

"I went through his computer, thoroughly. He doesn't want the police involved. He has his own secrets. He wouldn't go to them."

Good. Exactly as we practiced.

"Lief!" My father barks. "You saw the envelope. What does it mean?"

"I wait until I receive an order," Lief says, calm as ever. He looks at his nails for a moment. "I did not receive an order."

My father rolls up his sleeves. "I don't appreciate disobedience."

"I cleared him," I say firmly. "Mr. Smith is clean. If Lief would have gotten involved, it would have led the police to our doorstep. He has a family. He keeps detailed records of his clients. Do you really think they wouldn't have questions?"

Still, my father punches me, harder than I would have expected. I stare at the ground while trying to clear the stars from my vision. Old, yes. Frail, fuck no. I click my jaw back into place, actually happy that I got in that fight that fucked it up way back when.

Meeting his eyes, I ignore the blood in my mouth and arch an eyebrow. He's still fuming. Chase bangs his hands on the table. "If you don't trust what I can do then why fucking employ me at all?"

That pulls attention his way. He seethes as he looks at our father. "Your tactics are going to bite us in the ass with the way the world is now. We got answers from Stefan and made sure he won't be an immediate issue. We handled this look into the leak!"

Sven, fathers right hand man, just watches us from by the door.

I see blood when I pull my hand from my mouth. "Bloodshed doesn't fix every problem. It's not fixing the issue with the leak. An investigation – done correctly – will."

I don't point out how many lives it will save, how many families will be able to stay together, how many sons and daughters will be able to go to college without the temptation to run to us for help only to be dragged into this fucking business.

They can do better and if all I can do is give them a chance, I'm going to. I didn't forget every lesson my mother tried to teach me as a child.

My father sits and laughs once. "Well, if you're so convinced, who else could it be?"

"Someone who knows more than the money shit," Chase says clearly. "Someone who knows everything about the organization and has everything to lose."

My eyes flick around the room and I swear I see Sven's lips turn down slightly. I switch to Russian and nod to him. "And you. What do you think?"

"Not my job to think."

Lief nods in agreement. "But it must be someone on the inside. Not everyone knows about the dirty business."

"I know my system isn't bugged and I can spot a virus or spyware on a computer." Chase continues, switching all of us back to English. "Mr. Smith couldn't have known about anything that goes on in this building."

"It sounds like I should have Lief interrogating you two." My father cracks his knuckles. "Especially with this blatant show of weakness and disrespect."

"I protected us." I hiss. "Even if you don't see it, even if you don't care that everything could go up in flames around you. I kept the police away. I kept a good accountant. I kept our organization functioning for another day."

Father scoffs. "Barely."

Sven says something in Father's ear and he nods. "Get out of my sight, boys. Lief ... stay. You're needed."

Lief doesn't say anything to that, but his eyes stay on me. He dips his chin ever so slightly and I appreciate the solidarity. My father may have taken him in when he had limited prospects out of college, but loyalty isn't bought. It's formed.

Chase tugs on my shirt. "What about that?"

"I trust Lief. Do you?" I ask, wanting a real answer.

He rubs the back of his neck. "Enough. I trust him enough."

"I have to go make an appointment to satisfy our father," I grumble. "To deal with my apparent weakness."

Chase swallows. "I'm not available on Saturday. Make that clear."

"Of course." I wave my hand. "Enjoy your time with our girl."

"How did … never mind." He heads in his own direction.

I go to my office and set up an appointment with said woman. Valerie's name doesn't have a place in this house unless we're sure we're alone. Just like I know she won't consider an appointment with me if I use my own name.

So I smile when I'm asked and say my name is Herald Vance. Chase gets her this weekend, but I'll have her latest appointment Thursday and remind her what she's missing out on while checking off a box for father.

VALERIE

*C*hase was right, I survive the week. Which means I wait for him Saturday in a white sundress with watercolor flowers printed on it. He shows up in some kind of luxury car that makes my baby look like she belongs in a junkyard.

I get in before he can get out and see he's unbuckled. Shaking my head, I lean over him, meeting his eyes, and click his seatbelt in place. "Be safe for me, Chase."

"If only you knew what I did in my spare time." He chuckles.

I cup his cheek in my hand. He's so damn rebellious, so eager to prove that he's better than the average man, that he's invincible, perfect. I prefer when he's just him. His eyes widen as I keep stroking his cheek gently.

"Stay safe so we can go on more dates," I murmur before kissing him softly.

When I sit back down, he nods slowly. "Ready for our date?"

"The one that's definitely *not* the dinner cruise?"

"You asked for no paparazzi. I aim to please." He pulls on sunglasses to beat the steady dropping of the sun and I shake my head as I buckle myself into place.

Of course, Chase drives like a crazy person until I order him, using that damn mom voice that Sophie's always given me shit about, to slow the fuck down. He obeys immediately, reaching over to take my hand and press it to his mouth.

"Don't like fast cars?"

"I don't trust the other people on the road," I pant, shaking slightly. "You're a wild child."

"I know you're not all talk, Valerie." He chuckles. "I'll learn your limits."

"Quickly," I hiss.

We get to a marina and Chase pauses for a moment, glancing around, then nods. "Feel like a race to the dock?"

"Is everything about speed with you?" I demand.

But with his hand in mine, we half-sprint, half-trip to the dock. I bend over a little to catch my breath. I clearly need more time in the gym to keep up with these three. I stand and rub the back of my neck. My hair's already falling out of my bun and whipping around my face as Chase leads me past luxury sailboats and fishing boats to the second to last branch off the dock.

He waves his hands to a yacht. A gorgeous yacht, actually. "This is my girl."

"Lovely," I say with an approving nod.

He helps me board the yacht and before I can really get my bearings, we're leaving the marina and heading onto the Potomac River.

Sitting on the deck, where there's a single table set up, Chase finally removes his sunglasses. He's dressed impeccably, as always, his suit perfectly tailored to show off that hard body he has underneath. Remembering he's older than me and has this much energy, this much fun gives me hope for the future.

He takes my hand and brushes his thumb over my wrist. "We're on a boat with dinner, I think I stayed in the lines pretty closely."

"You didn't need to bid on something to ask me out," I mumble. "You could have just asked me out. Anytime since the wedding."

"You could have texted too," He says.

"I made the first move," I remind him. "Pulled you up to my room and everything. It was your job to make the second one."

"Sorry that I didn't receive an instruction manual on how to do this." He kisses my fingers softly.

"Dating's new to you?" I ask, trying to be somewhat coy and avoid throwing myself.

His lips lift at the corner, ever so softly. It warms his whole face and I can't believe he's more than thirty with that mix of 'kid caught in the cookie jar' and absolute joy etched in his features.

"You make all the rules for relationships and dating that I know useless," He says. When I arch my eyebrow at that *maybe* compliment, he continues. "Sex first normally means a one-night stand. You're younger than any woman I've dated since I was well … thirty, and you like being the one in charge."

I'm still waiting for that not to head into insult territory.

"You're exciting and different from every dating guide I've ever seen and trust me, I read a lot of them as a kid."

My hand tightens on his. "Had trouble?"

"I had a hot older brother that loved to fight my battles for me while I was pudgy, nerdy, and lived for videogames and the budding field of coding." He snorts.

Standing, I walk around the table to sit on his lap. Chase drapes his arm around me as I nuzzle his neck. "Computers are sexy."

"Now they are," He grumbles.

I rub over his chest, undoing two of the buttons to tease him, and come to a stop when a server walks onto the deck. Trying to scramble out of Chase's lap so I don't look like a complete bimbo, only means he holds me tighter.

He motions to the table. "Please."

The man drinks me in, staring obviously at my cleavage and Chase gives him a deadly glare. "Something you wanted to say about dinner or are you fishing for a pink slip?"

The waiter apologizes and rushes away.

"That was mean," I chide.

"He was eye-fucking you." Chase kisses my jaw, following the curve up to my ear. "That's my job."

I squirm at that delicious sense of possessiveness.

Chase reaches over me and offers me a fork of something dripping and glistening with butter. "Better eat it before we make a mess."

My mouth wraps around the food and I suck the fork to avoid staining the one white dress I have. The flavor is amazing. I swallow and stare at the plate. "What is it?"

"Escargot. Covered in garlic and herb butter with parmesan melted on top. Do you like it?"

I nod, then steal the fork and reach over to put two on the tongs before offering it to Chase. He slowly opens his mouth and I slide the food in. He bites down without ever looking away from me.

He lets me feed him most of the meal, but when the main course comes, Chase folds my arms over my chest, holding my hands as I stare, open-mouthed at the stuffed lobster. Chase kisses my throat softly.

"Delicious."

I nod. "I'm suddenly starving."

"You'll have to wait." He whispers in my ear before biting my neck. "I want you before the meal."

"Chase," I groan. "There are people around."

He adjusts so he's holding both my hands behind my back with one hand and slowly rubs up along the inside of my thigh. His fingers are featherlight as they stroke up and down but constantly move closer to my underwear.

I whimper and squirm against him, feeling him harden behind me. "Fuck."

"What do you think, baby? Think you can come quietly?" His fingers push against my panties. "That you can get off without anyone noticing?"

"No." I gasp as my head falls back over his shoulder. I press my lips to his neck. "I don't want to be interrupted again."

He considers that while drawing lazy circles over my clit. He hums in his throat. "I think we should try."

"But!"

The word dies on my tongue as he pushes my underwear to the side to stroke from my entrance to my clit and back slowly, two fingers spreading around my clit and giving me a *tease* of what I could have.

"Chase," I groan, rolling my hips against him.

"I think you want to try," He croons. "Try to be quiet."

I nod. "Yes. So much."

Chase rubs my clit in fast circles, then pushes his fingers inside me, rubbing deep inside me in a pattern that drive me insane. My lips part, but then I bite my bottom lip, trying to be quiet. I turn and hide my face in his neck.

"Chase, yes. So …" Words flee from my brain as chase pushes his fingers deeper inside me. His other hand strokes up my belly then circles my nipple through my dress. I shudder and arch into his hand as my nipple hardens. "Fuck."

"Better be quiet. Otherwise my hands will be busy decking that waiter," He growls.

I bite his neck to stop the dirty moan from leaving my throat. I take everything he gives, groaning and whimpering against his throat as his hand pushes down the top of my dress to cup my breast and squeeze my nipple before rolling it between his fingers.

He feels so good, and he's so hard under me that I still feel unsatisfied while getting closer and closer to the edge. Heat teases my toes, curling them, as I struggle, wanting to cover my mouth to stay silent, but Chase has me pinned so tightly against him, that I can't move.

He pushes his fingers all the way inside me, fucking me harder and faster with his fingers and then I come apart, my legs shaking and nearly biting through my bottom lip so we're not interrupted. My pussy squeezes around Chase's fingers and another little thrill teases my body.

I twitch as Chase frees his finger, then he sucks them, licking and groaning around his fingers. I meet his eyes and claim a kiss as soon as his fingers are free. I grip the back of his neck and crush him against me, licking along his tongue and tasting myself on his mouth.

Groaning, I kiss him harder, deeper.

The clinking of ice pulls me away and I see the waiter, now very flushed refilling our wine glasses before walking away. Chase chuckles. "You were naughty."

"I was quiet." I tap his nose, then kiss him again. "Now, be good and feed me."

He grins and does exactly as I ask, feeding me the beyond delicious lobster. It's the most expensive meal I've ever had and with Chase punctuating every two to three bites with a kiss, it's even better. I take his fork and try to feed him, but he grabs my wrist.

"I can feed myself," He argues.

"Oh, sorry, am I threatening your masculinity?" I arch an eyebrow and take the food from the fork.

He groans and adjusts me on his lap and rubs himself against me. "I'm *very* confident in the masculinity that matters."

"Well if you're eating, then what will I be doing?"

He watches me sink to the ground between his legs. "You should order those waiters to stay away."

He waves his hand once and I unzip his slacks. He groans as I drag his pants and boxers down to his knees so I can wrap my mouth around something even better than the food in front of us.

Chase bundles my now loose hair in his hands and guides me as I suck and lick his cock. He groans and thrusts into my mouth. He holds me in place, not letting me have control. He fucks my throat, his cock filling my mouth over and over again as my eyes water and I groan.

My whole body goes to jelly. How am I going to be able to handle this on repeat? It's too hot. I shiver and squeeze my thighs together as I grip his thighs and lick him faster while sucking hard. Chase groans and rolls his hips, hitting the back of my throat.

My eyes roll back as he uses me like he needs until he comes down my throat with a low moan. He shakes as I suck him gently, swirling my tongue around the head to get every drop of him before he releases my hair.

He rubs over my bottom lip and pushes his thumb into my mouth so I suck it clean. When he pulls his thumb back he shakes his head. "Like I said, you're impossible to plan for, Valerie."

CHASE

*V*alerie puts my clothes back together, then kisses me softly. I clean up her makeup and cuddle her close. "Holy fuck, woman. Was that too rough?"

"No." She rubs her lips across my jaw. "It was so good."

I shiver. How is she so … perfect? Maddening, wild, yet submissive? The combination is just too intense. She turns my face to steal a kiss, then loads up a fork and feeds me. I roll my eyes. There's something about being fed by her that is … embarrassing.

I steal the fork from her again. "Valerie."

"Let me take care of you," She says seriously. "Just because you have money and just because you're the man … that doesn't mean that you don't need some softness too."

I just blink at her stupidly. "What?"

She rolls her eyes and gets up to stand behind me, massaging my shoulders until I'm sure I'm going to die of pure happiness. "Just relax. Enjoy your lobster and let me make you feel good."

"You just did."

"And I'm going to keep doing it," She purrs in my ear. "And you're going to tell me about you -the kind of things I can't find on Google."

I groan and lean into her hands. "My mom left when I was five. Hunter and I lived with my uncle for a while, until we hit high school, then our dad took over. He's a piece of shit."

"How so?"

I have to skirt the line. But her fingers, kneading into my tight muscle feels so good. "I'd rather not talk about him. We're not in your office."

She laughs softly. "Then what would you rather talk about?"

I tell her about the coding programs I've been able to put together to catch and pause any kind of data breach for our company. I tell her about my strange love for snakes and how I've always wanted to have one, but Hunter is terrified of them. I tell her about how much I love pointing out problems with mafia movies and spy movies. That I'm horrible to watch movies with because I like pointing out problems and adding to them.

"You left out some things," Valerie says softly in my ear. "How sweet you can be. How thoughtful you are."

I close my eyes. "Valerie, don't just compliment me."

"You're also a dense asshole who can't see when someone wants you to text them and make a move."

I chuckle and slide my hands over hers. "Have some wine, baby. I spent a lot of time choosing the right one for you."

She sits back in her chair and takes a slow drink, her dark eyes on mine. She licks over her bottom lip and then eyes me hungrily. "Are you my dessert?"

"Maybe." I chuckle.

We take the wine to the plush seats on the yacht and watch the sunset together while she tells me about how she likes sarcasm and misunderstandings in TV shows. She loves documentaries more than anything because she likes to learn, but she's also a sucker for Rom-Coms, especially the whole enemies to lovers thing even though it's everywhere now.

"Anything else?" I ask, finishing my glass while hooking my arm around her leg and drawing her closer, so she's nearly in my lap.

"I don't know what to do with you, Hunter, and Lief. I've never done something like this and Sophie makes it look so easy, but I'm worried about you all getting jealous and taking it out on me, or fighting, or something like that." She takes a long drink. "Or, being seen with all three of you in public, with you, then Hunter, and people trying to dig deep into my life."

"You have secrets?" I tease. "What kind?"

"I *don't* have secrets," She corrects. "I am myself, always, whatever version comes out, even the prickly cactus version. But I have clients and my future business is going to depend on my reputation. If I'm in the tabloids constantly, who's going to come to get life advice from me?"

She shakes her head and looks over the water. "I've never been on this river before. Or a yacht."

I rub up her thigh, then jerk her closer. "So you haven't had sex on a boat before?"

Her eyes flick to mine and she smirks. "I haven't. Are you going to change that?"

"There is a bed downstairs." I hint.

With that, she stands up and offers me her hand. "I'm not in the habit of waiting for what I want. I take it. And I'm taking you, now."

I groan and lead her down to the private room. I lock the door and watch as she strips slowly, unzipping her dress, then dropping it around her ankles. She only has a thong on. Valerie takes one step back, then another, leaving her heels on as she hooks her fingers in her thong and edges it down until her thong drops between her heels too.

I toss my jacket as I watch her lay across the bed, gripping the sheets and arching her back like she's offering her ass. She rolls on her side and strokes over her breasts, along her belly, then her thigh, spreading her legs to show me everything she's offering.

"Fucking hell, baby. Do you have any idea how much I want you?"

"Show me," She orders. "Better hurry before I get myself finished."

I rip my clothes off and join her on the bed.

I grip her full breasts in my hands and lick over her nipple hungrily before wrapping my mouth around the hard peak and sucking. The other one demands my attention and I can't stop myself from doing the same on that side before kissing and biting down her belly as she rolls her body against mine.

I push her legs wide and lick over her clit. She's still wet for me. I pull her tighter against my mouth and feast on her pussy. She moans and drops her head to the bed as she grips the sheets tightly. I squeeze her breast in one hand, then pinch her nipple, rolling it as she pants and whimpers, rolling her body against my mouth.

Before she can come, I lick up her side and kiss her with passion. She sits up, reaching between us to stroke over my cock, and says, "Fuck me hard, Chase. No restraint."

As if restraint is possible with her. She rubs up my chest and kisses me hungrily as she continues rubbing over my cock, teasing me with those light touches until she guides me to her pussy. I lift her legs, dropping her back, and squeeze her legs together as I thrust into her.

"Oh, fuck yes. That feels so good," She pants.

I climb on top of her, both her ankles bumping over my shoulder, the heels scraping against each other. She moans and pants as I fuck her hard and deep. But I'm not close enough, it's not enough. I spread her legs and push her knees to her shoulders.

Her eyes roll back and she wiggles against me as I get even deeper at this angle. I bite across her chest before sucking her nipple between my lips. She groans and pants. She's so wet I can hear it with each thrust and it's driving me insane, she's driving me insane.

"Fuck, Chase!" She yells.

She comes hard for me, screaming and howling until I'm sure the whole river knows that she's coming apart. Then we change positions and go again. And again. I want her every way I can have her. I grip her hair hard, jerking her back so she has to brace on her hands and knees. My other hand guides her hips as I fuck her hard and deep.

It's too much, she's too much. So tight, so hot, so fucking good. I kiss across her back, then get to the top curve of her ass and softly bite it. She whimpers and moans. We're slippery and hot and god damn, she's perfect. I shove her forward, then lay behind her, lifting her leg so I can fuck her from behind. She moans and nods.

"God, you're good," She moans. "So fucking good."

I finger her clit as I fuck her and she comes apart again, soaking the sheets under us. As her pussy quivers and tightens around me, clutching my cock deep inside her, I can't hold out anymore. I come and bite the back of her neck, growling and groaning as I finish, wrapping my leg around her hip and keeping her close.

"Holy shit," She pants as she keeps trembling with my cock still inside her.

It's the most intense sex I've ever had. Those damn whispered compliments and encouragements, the promise that I'm not too rough, that she's not breakable, the positions, the way I edged myself every time we switched positions, all of it was too much.

I trail my fingertips over her side and she shivers.

"Chase," She presses back against me. "I like your yacht."

"Yeah?" I rasp against her shoulder. "Just the yacht?"

"I like you too," She hums. "And the way you fuck me."

I chuckle and collar her throat before turning her to face me so I can kiss her again. She grinds against me. "How long are you keeping me?"

"As long as I can have you," I purr in her ear. "Especially all to myself."

She rolls, as I slide out of her and she kisses over my throat softly while rubbing my back. "Then we're going to cuddle, clean up, and have sex at least one more time."

I lift her mouth from my skin to kiss her again, hungry and demanding until she softens every curl of my tongue and every lick. She kisses me lazily, like we have plenty of time and for the first time … I feel like we do.

Nothing outside of this boat matters. My father, my family, the organization, none of it can touch us here. Valerie rubs over my bottom lip. "You don't have to rush with me, Chase. Or hide. Or work so hard to impress me."

I open my mouth to argue, but she kisses me again. "You don't because I like who you are when we're together." Another kiss. "When you're you. You're an amazing man and you don't owe anyone proof of that."

I shudder and hug her tightly, pressing my face to her hair. She doesn't have a fucking clue the shit I'm involved in, the way I deal with the life I have, she doesn't know anything, but that validation felt so good I don't want to bring it up either.

She rubs over my sides and kisses my shoulder. "I mean it. You're wonderful. In and out of bed."

I cup her face between my hands and shake my head. What the fuck am I supposed to say to that. She's young, beautiful, smart as a whip, and … and she's mine. I take an unsteady breath as my heart throbs in my chest.

"You better prepare for a hell of a night, baby." I breathe. "In and out of bed."

She brushes her fingers through my hair and kisses across my throat as I stroke over her arm. I can't touch her enough. Can't get enough time with her and I feel like I'm hanging on her silence, waiting for what's going to break it.

Valerie grins and I see that mischievous glow in her eyes. "Wow me, baby boy."

VALERIE

hen I leave the yacht with Chase, my legs are boneless. He ends up carrying me back to his car, but we manage to avoid the press, for now. As soon as he heads out of the lot, I see them converge, trying to get a picture of us.

I shake my head at him, but I'm barely awake, even after the short nap we had. Chase rubs over my thigh. "Feeling good, baby?"

"More satisfied than I thought possible." I hum, then look over at Chase. He beams. I rub his jaw. "You look pretty happy yourself."

"Let's see, I caught the girl who got away. I'm thrilled."

I giggle and shake my head at him. "When am I going to get to see you again?"

He nearly misses a red light. I gasp and find his eyes on me. "Seriously? I don't have to beg?"

I shake my head. "I want more of this conversation thing … and the sex doesn't hurt at all."

He beams. "As soon as you want me, gorgeous. We'll find time in our lives for each other."

"I'm glad you're not asking me to leave my job."

"Never."

"Or school."

He shakes his head. "You have gotten to choose the life you want to live and you're making it happen. It's sexy as hell."

I kiss him again before hopping out of his car and running inside. He takes off, making sure the press follows him instead of me. I laugh to myself and stumble up the stairs and into my apartment.

Yeah, I'm going to have to join a gym to keep up with them. My abs hurt, my body aches in the best way, and I just can't believe I got off a luxury yacht after having the best meal of my life and some of the best sex the world has to offer.

Chase is unforgettable.

Before I know it, I'm texting him and Lief regularly every day and Hunter when the urge strikes – mainly meaning when I want to tease. But then Thursday rolls around and after two patients, I see a new one on the schedule, taking up the last appointment.

Herald Vance? Who the hell …

My intercom buzzes. "Valerie, your four o'clock is here."

"Thanks. Be right there."

I walk out, looking at the documents submitted. Family stress, anger and impulse control, coping mechanisms. An interesting mix. I lift my head and see only one man sitting in the waiting room. One man I don't want to see. Short dark curly hair, hazel eyes, a smirk teasing his lips as he watches my reaction.

Hunter.

I motion him forward. "Mr. Vance."

"Dr."

As we walk along the hallway, I shake my head. "Not a doctor yet. Just Valerie."

I stop him before I open the door to my office and shove the clipboard against his chest. I lower my voice. "My office is a professional space, is that understood? No flirting, no sexual bullshit. This is my *career*. Understand?"

"Yes, Valerie." He says, not even attempting to touch me. "For the whole hour-"

"Fifty minutes."

"I will control myself. I'm here with a purpose," He insists.

I measure him up again. He's sexy, tall, and imposing, but there's some kind of softening on his normally unyielding edges. I nod and open the door. I motion to the chair and sit across from him, right against the window.

He taps his fingers on the chair as I look over the clipboard again. I rub my forehead. "Using a fake name isn't very ethical."

"You would have kicked me off the schedule and I need to be able to trust the person I tell all my secrets to."

I nod and motion him to go ahead. "What do you want to talk about today?"

"My father." His eyes flick up to me with that signature smirk. "Unless that's too on the nose."

I arch an eyebrow. We're not doing his stupid cocky bullshit right now. He either talks or he doesn't but either way, this is a serious environment and it's staying that way. Hunter gives up with a roll of his eyes.

126

"He thinks I'm weak. Suggested counseling to fix my issues."

"And what do you think?" I ask.

His eyes meet mine and I see the briefest flash of surprise. "I think my father would love any excuse to commit me when I don't meet his expectations. He thinks every decision is life and death and so if I offer another way, considering anyone but our direct family or share-holders, I'm out of line, disobedient, or an embarrassment."

"And what do you think about yourself." I rephrase.

He considers that, rubbing his chin. Then he talks in circles. About how he wants to do things a different way, and how important it is for companies, people, and morals to change with the times and with the situation. How not everything can be solved with a cutthroat attitude and then he slumps. He says he's tired of pretending to be someone he's not, that he's tired of not having control over his life, and how he doesn't even get a say in what he does with his time. Like he's living someone else's life and only gets the smallest input.

I keep watching him.

Hunter swallows. "I think I'm fine other than that. I think that things need to change in the business and that showing some regard for other people is a good thing, not a sign of weakness. I think ..." His fingers trail over his bottom lip as he watches me. "I think, if anything, I should push for more freedom."

"Then why don't you?"

"It's not as easy as it sounds, sweetheart."

I don't bother to correct the nickname.

Not when he leans forward with his face covered. "I'm forty-two and still taking orders from my father like they're law. How pathetic is that?"

"It's not pathetic." I make a note about his constant negative self-talk. "It's a survival mechanism."

"What?"

"You mentioned that he came into your life when you were in high school, right?"

Hunter nods. "Yeah. He took over when our uncle left. Father is a mean son of a bitch too. Every rule break comes with violence. But I don't want to be pitied. I could take him if I needed to. But ..." he looks to the side. "I worry about my brother."

"Your brother, who's also a grown man and able to take care of himself," I remind him. I take a slow breath. "You learned to obey or to disobey in the ways that show you're willing to listen to survive the sudden change to make sure that you could protect yourself. That's not weakness, Hunter."

His eyes raise to mine.

"That's understanding life. The only issue I see here is that you are willing to forgo control over what you want, you're willing to give up the life you *could* have because you are afraid of the very real consequences of those actions. When you work with family, it's nearly impossible to get real work-life balance because everything circles around until it feels ..."

"I feel trapped," He whispers. "I work almost seven days a week and I never have a full day, a full weekend to myself. It's selfish to want time to do anything other than protect others – our business – and give them the opportunities I didn't have."

"Why do you feel like that's on your shoulders alone?" I ask. "Why can no one else take care of that for the weekend?"

He gapes at me, tries twice for an answer, and shakes his head. "Because they are stuck in the old ways and if I don't control it, it will spiral somewhere else. And if I connect with someone, really connect with them…"

Now I feel him looking into my soul. Not as a counselor, as me. My body heats as electricity ripples between us. I can't look away from his eyes, can't pull myself out of his unfinished sentence.

"If I was to take a chance and be real with someone and show them what's under the jokes and flirting, they'd leave."

"Why?" My voice shakes.

"My life is pretty on the outside, enchanted, but it's ugly on the inside. Violent, hard, unforgiving. And it's turned me into a monster, even though I fight it every day."

I shift forward in my seat. "You're afraid that if you showed someone who you really are, they'd push you away? That they wouldn't be able to love you, or even like you?"

"I'm sure of it. My mother left my father for those reasons. He became different when he took over the company. I'm going to have to take over. And whoever I love will leave me too, because I'm an ugly beast, or worse … I'm a man who wants what he doesn't deserve, will do everything to have it, then ruin it by dragging it into my life when I know the consequences."

Shivering, I look at the time. We have a whole five minutes left. "If you look at someone like an object, yes. But people have their own motives, their own feelings, their own wants. Trying to read minds doesn't do anyone any good. Maybe someone, just someone is more interested in the real Hunter underneath the mask."

He shifts in his seat, then stands. His fingers nearly brush mine and I jump up, backing against my desk. "You promised. This is professional."

"Give me your professional answer then, Valerie. If you had the chance to show someone you could love, all the ugly things about you and the vulnerable things, to get real with them, but you knew it could end badly … would it be selfish to try?"

"That depends on your intent."

"How?" He takes another step for me and I can feel my skin sizzle under that gaze.

I choke down a ragged breath. "Do you really want to involve her? Take the chance to hurt her? Do you *know* that you'll ruin her, or is that a guess? Are you willing – if she falls for you, if she gives in – to catch her and fight for her? Or do you just want a good time?"

He licks across his bottom lip. "I would take every possible punishment to keep her from getting hurt. And right now, I'm more worried that she doesn't want to fall and that she definitely won't do the catching *when* I end up in love."

My mouth opens and closes a few times.

"What's your recommendation, Valerie? Do I shoot my shot and lay all the risk out? Show her everything I can offer, kink, banter, and the real stuff? Or do I cut my losses right here and now?"

I glance at the time. "Your session is done."

"Then you can really answer me, can't you?" He asks, stroking along the back of my arm. "The way you want to and not with your work voice."

"Show her everything. Don't spare the ugly stuff or the soft stuff. Be real … and she'd be willing to fall if things are right," I say softly.

Hunter leans toward me I shake my head, shrinking back. The office is open. "I'm still on the clock and the front door is open. Professional. There are rules."

He watches as I type some notes into my computer, clock out, then lock the front door. I slowly turn around and see him waiting there, leaning against the edge of the hallway. He arches an eyebrow.

I swallow hard as I approach him. "Now we can leave."

"I'm impatient." He growls, grabbing me and pushing me against the wall before wrapping his hand around my throat. His knee pushes between my thighs and he raises it so every time I squirm, the friction between my legs builds. He holds his lips just out of reach before kissing along my jaw and to my ear.

"I'm shooting my shot. Are you in the mood to play?" I can already feel him hard against my hip.

Shivering, I face him and my lips brush his as I speak. "Show me everything or there's no way I'm begging."

LIEF

"*L*ief." Mr. Volkov walks around me. I glance at the time quickly, making note of how much longer our meetings have been recently. It's only three in the afternoon. "I'd like to speak to you about my sons."

My eyes steady on him. I don't like the undercurrent in his voice. It promises violence. Where my best friends are concerned, I like to be clear. I spare them the details about what I do here. I spare them the details about my life. That is the only way our friendship works.

I can't break the trust we've grown.

"Where is Hunter today?"

Mr. Volkov waves at the air. "At counseling or something. I'm trying to get him back on the same page and I'm sure talking out all those weaknesses and fantasies will remove the distraction."

He's wrong if he sent his son to counseling. I'm sure he's with Valerie. And I'm sure they're not doing any professional talking if Hunter is getting his way. He always gets his way.

"This meeting is for the two of us specifically." Mr. Volkov sits and folds his hands together on the table. "I need you to watch out for my boys. You do an excellent job of keeping problems at bay with your … skills."

My arm tightens in response.

"If only they know that each additional tattoo you get is a marker of more." He chuckles. "But you must understand you serve me. I took you in. I have given you a comfortable life. Any friendship you have with them could distract you."

Distraction is bad in this world. I've learned it quickly.

The door opens and Sven walks in, standing by the door. My eyes narrow. He's been uncomfortably involved in too many of these conversations without his own opinions. And Sven has many opinions.

When he was training me, he shared them often. His eyes give up most of what he's feeling, but he's learned to school his face, at least around me.

"Sven and I have been trying to further investigate this leak and I believe it's a bigger issue than my sons are willing to face. I believe Hunter is too weak to take the necessary steps. Yes, Mr. Smith was cleared thanks to Chase and our interrogation, but next time, we may not be so lucky."

He doesn't expect or want an answer, so I don't give one.

"You are stronger than either of them. You know what this company truly rests on and the risks that *cannot* be allowed. My sons are skirting those lines. They get to have their fun, their time in the papers, and their time with women. But I have noticed a change in them both."

Sven nods.

"Chase has always been willful and eager to prove himself, but he is bordering on defiant. Hunter is pushing ... too far." Sven agrees. "We cannot trust he will wait for his inheritance."

"I expect you to keep a close eye on both of them and report accordingly. I will handle the leak on my own. Do not do any further investigating. Do not assist my boys with any investigating. If they give you orders, bring it to me first." Mr. Volkov lists out new rules.

"Is this understood?"

"It is," I say simply.

Mr. Volkov grins and Sven pours him Vodka before pouring me a glass as well. We both drink and the conversation continues. Mr. Volkov likes to have those he's speaking to a little bit buzzed. He believes it loosens their tongue.

I've been drinking since I was sixteen and I am larger than he is. He's fighting an uphill battle if he thinks that method will work on me, but I don't see the merit in pointing it out. He goes over – in detail – the expectations he has of me again.

I am to be completely available to him no matter the time and nothing is to be more important than his orders. Nothing and no one. His sons included. He gets through another round of saying the same thing until Sven leans forward.

"Ah. Thank you, Sven." Mr. Volkov nods. "Sven has noticed that my boys have been talking about a woman. They do not use her name and they seem to be seeing the same one. Monitor this. If she becomes a distraction, simply pay her off. No woman is going to prioritize my boys over the money."

He doesn't know the woman. But I keep my face even despite the smirk pulling at my lips. If I was to offer Valerie money to stay away from us, she'd become the biggest problem this company has ever seen, just to prove that she's not able to be bought.

It's endearing.

I'd love to watch her destroy all of Mr. Volkov's methods, his rules, and his control with one curl of her finger or one whispered sentence in Hunter's ear. She wouldn't control any of us, not intentionally outside the bedroom, but she'd get in our heads.

Just like that, I miss being inside her. I'm going to need to borrow her soon, just a chunk of time to remind her I'm not all talk and not just some man at the other end of a phone. I'm overdue to let her take care of me.

"Lief!"

I blink twice and refocus on Volkov. "Do you understand? I don't want anyone, let alone some piece of ass distracting you or my boys. When you three committed to this organization, that meant giving up any illusions of having a normal life. Is that clear?"

"Yes."

"Good. Then we understand each other." He glances at the time. "Hunter's appointment starts at four. Make sure he gets home without fucking every broken woman at the office, please."

I nod, but as I go to the garage, I see Chase. He's pleased as can be and has been since he got back Saturday. I incline my head to him and he comes over. "We can trust you, right? We're not misguided in *that* respect, are we?"

"Yes and no," I answer. "In that order."

He nods. "You know where Hunter is today, right?"

I dip my chin.

"Then you know that Dad doesn't want him there a second longer than necessary." Chase gets closer to me. "Let's give Hunter one hour with her. I think that's the least we can do … after counseling. It's such an easy building to miss. And with so many people around, he can be difficult to grab."

"The first counseling session is normally ninety minutes, isn't it?" I ask, playing along with his game. "To ensure a clear baseline, signing the necessary paperwork. And Hunter is a gentleman, he would never allow a woman to stay alone at an office without walking her to her car."

Chase pats my shoulder. "Good man."

"We will need to talk about your continued snooping into Mr. Smith's file," I say clearly. "Your father doesn't approve and I am to report to him."

"I can turn the file over to you now then." Chase shrugs.

He hands me a manilla envelope and I make sure everything's there, but I'm not stupid enough to believe that Chase hasn't memorized what's important. I slip it in my coat and Chase follows me to my office where I put it in a safe.

Of course, my office has no camera either.

I glance at the time. 4:50. Hunter will be busy for another hour. I don't have a single doubt. Valerie may be making him work for her, but she wants him as much as she craved me when we were together.

"Our pet is worried about us," Chase informs me. "Thinks we're going to get jealous and take it out on her or fight each other."

I consider that a moment. I do care for the girl. More than just sex, she's intelligent, can hold interesting conversations, and seems to be able to mold herself to whatever a situation requires to be helpful while never hiding exactly what she thinks. That last add on to her personality makes it impossible for her to work in a place like this … but I don't feel the urge to demand answers from Chase or go and stop her from being with Hunter.

It's not the first time we've shared a woman. We're not inept when it comes to balancing our emotions. I think it would take all three of us to satisfy her constantly anyway.

"I have no issue," I say simply.

"Good. I wanted to prepare you since you're going to ensure Hunter is a good boy and comes home." Chase rolls his eyes. "When he does come home, I have news."

"And I have … a hunch," I simplify.

Sven has been at every meeting. He's changed in the last few months. He's gotten more leeway from Mr. Volkov and yet he's still everywhere. He pushed for Mr. Smith to be killed. He's been suspicious of the three of us.

I have a feeling he knows who the leak is and is covering.

Chase watches me carefully and nods. "I think we need to share something with Hunter. The three of us need to talk once he's able to focus on something other than … her."

"Impossible, but understood."

Chase nods and that leaves me free to go. I head out to the garage again, pick up my motorcycle since I know Hunter drove himself, and see the office location on my phone. There are two texts from Mr. Volkov asking why I haven't left to get his son. One threatening that if he leaves the office with anyone, it is me who will pay the price for insubordination.

He hasn't punished me since I first joined and let something slip to Hunter. Even then it was Sven who did the job. Back when Sven was larger, more muscular, more everything. Perhaps that's a fight I'd like to rehash.

I peel out of the mansion and get caught in five o'clock traffic. I don't bother weaving around the cars or rushing there. Instead, I text Hunter. I don't get a response by the second bout of traffic and I'm sure he's very busy and very focused on something much more important than his phone.

Valerie.

We should have never let things get this far with her. We shouldn't be protecting her. Per our jobs and our lives, we're only dragging her deeper into darkness without a flashlight. She doesn't know anything about what we do, who we are.

It's not fair to her.

I get to the office at nearly six p.m. and still see a light on inside, see Valerie's car and Hunter's. Of course, they're not close to done yet. Hunter has wanted her constantly and she's been denying him, teasing him, playing with him in her own way.

Now he's going to capitalize. I smirk and sit comfortably in the stretching shadows. I'll give them thirty minutes before I break-in.

Then we can see exactly how she'd handle two of us. See if she can hold her own in a relationship with multiple men before we even consider bringing her into our world of organized crime.

My phone dings again, Mr. Volkov asking what his son is doing.

I let him know that I have things taken care of and will be bringing him back tonight after a few words with him about his place in the company.

Or his place in bed, along with mine, sharing Valerie like he told her we would. That will count as words. My lips curl up at the thought and I park my bike before going to take a look at how strong the lock on the back door is.

VALERIE

*H*unter still has me against the wall, holding me in place like he has been for a full minute. And a minute has never felt this long. His lips skim my jaw and across my throat before his tongue flicks across the skin just above my raging pulse.

I squirm on his leg, building the friction further. "I think you're impatient, sweetheart."

"Hunter," I moan.

"I'm a generous man." He bites my earlobe before soothing it with a soft kiss. "All you have to do is beg and I'll give you everything. Everything I possibly can."

His words are fire lapping at my skin. I take a ragged breath and turn to meet his gaze. "I want you."

"I know you do." He chuckles. "How much?"

My pride tells me begging is weakness. But hunter frees one of his hands and skims along the neck of my shirt. I tremble and he snatches the fabric in his hand, jerking me forward against his hard body as his eyes flick down to take in my cleavage.

"How long do you want to wait before having me?" He demands.

I lick across my bottom lip and roll my hips on him. "You're the one dying for a taste. How long are you going to wait before stealing it?" I push him into one of the empty conference rooms and lock the door. Because I have a feeling we cannot wait another minute to have each other.

He groans and presses his forehead to mine. I feel each puff of his breath across my face and can't help but lean back, lips parted. His lips ghost across mine in something too soft to be a kiss, then I feel the words form.

"Beg me, Valerie."

"Please?" My brain is fried trying to resist him. My pride is shaky. The need building low in my belly has control. "Kiss me, Hunter. Please."

He chuckles softly and kisses the corner of my mouth. "Better, but not good enough, beautiful."

I moan and rub myself across his thigh. "Please! I need to feel your mouth on mine. Need you to touch me. I fantasize about you fucking me. I need it. Please. Please."

"Good girl," He purrs.

The words make me giddy, eager to please, eager to do more. But before I can do anything, his mouth crashes down on mine. There's nothing soft about Hunter, the way he kisses, the way he owns me.

He claims me in a soul-searching kiss that curls my toes and drops one of my heels to the floor. All I can do is take him. His tongue plundering my mouth, his hard body grinding against mine, his teeth nipping my bottom lip.

And then he draws back, looks at me, changes the angle and kisses me again. I rub myself against him like a needy cat, trying desperately to get more, to cling to him, to get some kind of control, but I can't.

Our kisses are warfare and I'm not sure I can survive the onslaught that has me shaking and eager for more. So I give in, licking across his tongue, moaning, trying to prolong every kiss and make the most of him.

I want to memorize the way he smells like old books and spiced leather. How he tastes like the best treat. How sexy and silky his tongue is against mine.

He jerks back and looks around like he wants to put me somewhere. I shake my head and manage to pull my arms free so I can wrap them around his neck, digging my fingers through his silky hair. "Now. Fuck me right now."

He chuckles but doesn't pull away from the kiss I give him as I dig my nails into his back and scalp. Hunter sinks with me to the floor and drags my shirt up my body before tearing it off. "Better hope there aren't cameras in here."

"Turned them all off accidentally," I pant. "Whoops."

Groaning, he looks me over as I struggle with his shirt. I get through four of the buttons before I jerk it over his head to see the expanse of tan skin. I marvel at him. How is he so fucking perfect? Every sculpted inch of his body and that one tattoo that I think his brother has too.

Hunter grabs my hand and holds it down above my head, his fingers lacing through mine. "You're a wicked little thing."

"I want to touch you." I pant. "I want to fuck you and blow you. I want everything."

He blinks a few times, as if he didn't expect that, then lets out a slew of words in a language I don't know before kissing me like he can pour his life into mine that easily. Groaning, I take it all. I tighten my grasp on his hand while my fingers dance along his spine and down to his tight, delicious ass.

Hunter sits up and strips me entirely, his eyes caressing me as they move across my body. "Fuck."

"Now who's begging for a taste." I tease.

"I don't beg." He growls.

And he proves it by kissing and licking down my body. I swear, there's not a place he doesn't taste before he buries his face between my legs. My back arches and I grab his head in both hands as I slide my legs over his shoulders.

He groans and jerks me closer, his hands sliding up my sides to cup my breasts and roll my nipples between his fingers. My eyes flutter shut as I release moan after whimpering moan. His mouth is wicked no matter how he uses it. I slap one hand down on the conference room carpet as my hips lift to rub against his tongue.

I catch his hungry gaze on me, demanding, sure, with that lingering spark of playfulness. And then he draws back, shoving my hips down. I whimper. I was so close to bliss, right on the edge. He pushes my hips down and licks up my body, from belly button to chin.

"You don't get to come yet, Valerie."

"But."

He rolls me over and smacks my ass. "I'm calling the shots right now, sweetheart. Are you going to be a good girl for me?"

I groan at that gravelly voice, "Yes."

"Give me whatever I want?" I hear the rustling of his clothes and look back to find him taking off his jeans.

I nod and wiggle my ass for him, just to earn another spank. "Yes."

"Get over here." He jerks me back to him as I giggle. He kisses and gently bites down my throat and to my shoulder. Palming my breast in one hand and fingering me with the other as I roll my body against the hardness under me. "Do you want me to fuck you?"

"Yes. Hard. Deep." Words are getting harder.

Lifting his hand from my breast to my throat, he squeezes lightly. "Show me."

I blink a few times. "What?"

"Put my cock inside you and show me what you want," He orders again.

I reach under myself to stroke over his length. I shiver and slide myself down inch by inch. We moan together and I adjust so I can ride him properly. Hunter groans and spreads my legs as he pushes his fingers tighter into my throat.

I feel a little light-headed, but it only makes everything more intense. The way he fills me so perfectly, how he hits every spot I need, the rumbling sounds that I feel leave his chest. So good. So perfect.

Why the fuck did I wait so long for this?

He bends me over, so I'm on my hands and knees and thrusts into me harder. I whimper and look back at him. The need and pleasure etched into every feature make him equal parts hot and scary at the same time.

"This what you've been craving, Valerie?"

"Yes." I pant, then grunt as he thrusts deep again.

I'm already seeing stars, but I'm afraid to say a word. I don't want to be edged again. I can't. I moan and bite my bottom lip hard as I close my eyes and let my body rock back against him with every roll of his hips.

"Such a good girl, sweetheart. Do you want to come?"

"Yes!" I yell, but it sounds like a plea.

He grips my hair tightly, pulling back. "Then let me hear everything that comes out of that beautiful mouth. Every sound you make for my cock, sweetheart."

"Fuck." I groan.

I don't hide a thing. I'm loud, give him all the dirty talk he could want, until my words clog in my throat and then Hunter swats my ass again. "Come. Now."

I can't resist. I fall over the edge and into an orgasm that consumes me, that has me nearly floating away if it weren't for Hunter's hand tugging on my hair. I whimper and let out another wild moan as I drop to my elbows.

Hunter draws back and rubs his cock over my clit, watching me shake as I calm myself from the intensity. "I think I'd like to hear that again, sweetheart."

"Now?" I ask, voice sticky.

"Yes."

He flips me over and pulls me back into his lap, sliding into my wet pussy easily. I grip his shoulders and kiss across his throat. He pants as he thrusts into me. I ride him slowly at first like a bull in a tavern, enjoying touching him, kissing him, finally having him.

He turns my head and kisses me hungrily as I move faster on him, bouncing and rolling my hips. Hunter tips my chin back. "I'll pull out when I'm close."

I shake my head. "I'm on the pill. Don't stop. Don't you fucking stop."

That seems to open up a whole different Hunter. He growls, rolls us so he's on top, and lifts one of my legs to pound into me harder and deeper. I whimper as he sucks my nipple between his lips and groans. Then he comes back up, fucking me so fast that I can't catch my bearings.

"Hunter!" I yell hoarsely.

"I'm not going to come inside you yet, sweetheart. You have to earn that. So when I'm ready, you're going to taste it."

"Yes." I pant, back arching again. "Yes, please!"

"Such a good girl for me," He groans, pounding into me at a rhythm I just can't handle. I whimper, grab at him, then come all over again.

He jerks out of me as I reach the highest peak of pleasure, then pulls me forward. I wrap my lips around his cock, tasting both of us at the same time as he fucks my throat. I moan and dig my fingers into his ass, loving how rough he is, loving how good he feels, how good he tastes.

"Fuck. Ready, Val?"

I nod and drag my tongue over his length. That's all it takes. He finishes in my throat and shudders, slowly drawing back, shaky inch by inch, until he collapses on the floor. He groans and strokes over my cheek. "Fuck, sweetheart you are good at that, Jesus."

I lick my bottom lip and hesitate before laying down with him. I'm not sure what's allowed. Chase loves cuddling. Lief is awkward as hell. And Hunter likes control, total and complete control.

Trembling, I start looking for my clothes, but he pulls me across his chest to play with my hair. His other hand strokes down my back. "You're worth the wait."

"Are you mad I made you wait?"

"More … curious." He lifts my chin and kisses me softly. "I knew you were into me. Knew you wanted me."

"I also hated your cocky asshole side." I tap his chest. "Even if it was funny sometimes."

His brow furrows.

145

"I like the real you, dummy," I whisper against his lips. "The one that was in my office. Intense, confused, unsure, vulnerable." I roll my eyes. "And still strong as hell."

Hunter shakes his head at me slowly, his nose brushing mine. "Why the hell would you like that?"

I rub over his chest. "Because it lets me know you're more than the average fuckboy."

He kisses me once, then twice, then again. This time, he's soft, gentle, like he's trying to find something in me. I carefully brush some hair from his face. Hunter rolls me onto my back and kisses my neck as his hand slides between my legs.

"You get to come again."

HUNTER

I lazily lick and suck Valerie's nipple while just rubbing her clit. She trembles and pants, whimpering softly as she gets closer. I switch to the other breast, trying to be soft after being so rough with her. The way she just says what she thinks bothers me and unnerves me.

How can she go from all riled and challenging to soft and honest like that without missing a beat? Why does it affect me so much?

"Hunter," She pants.

I push my fingers inside her and she writhes against me, rolling her body, panting, petting my hair until she soaks my fingers as she comes. But, since I don't feel like stopping, I don't. She groans and tries to dig her heels into the ground.

Her thighs tighten around my hand. "We should go."

"Mmm," I answer, flicking my tongue over her nipple while continuing. Her legs part again and she digs her fingers into her thigh just before she comes.

So fucking wet.

Before I can comment on how good she feels, I hear a beeping. Valerie sits up, pulls away from me, and stumbles to the computer in the corner. "Fuck. Someone just came in the back door."

She doesn't go for her clothes; she goes for her purse? Then out comes a taser. God damn, she truly is the sexiest woman on the planet. She doesn't expect me to save her and is all prepared to save herself, totally naked. Fuck she is hot.

I groan and her eyes flick to me before she picks up my shirt, puts it on, and opens the door, focusing on the dark hallway. She turns the thing on so it crackles, just before she's caught, turned and walked back into the lobby, the taser useless on the floor.

I smile at Lief I knew it was only a matter of time. "Father send you?"

"Of course," He murmurs, his eyes only on Valerie. She squirms a little until he kisses her temple. "Were you going to tase me, little viper?"

"You could have said something," She grumbles.

He chuckles softly and spins her around, kissing her hard and hungry as he strokes the back of her neck. I stroke my cock as I watch Lief devour her. Valerie tugs at his button up, presses herself tightly against him, shameless as ever.

"How long do we have?" I ask.

Lief draws back while Valerie paws at his shirt, steadily unbuttoning it. He thinks a moment. "Enough time."

I grin. Before our little minx can go for his pants, He turns her around and cups one of her breasts. "I missed you."

She looks up at him. "You're so hard to get a hold of." Then to me. "All of you."

"And you want all of us, sweetheart?" I ask.

She nods. "Yes. I'm greedy."

"I think we should punish you for that." I chuckle, motioning her forward.

She takes a step toward me and lets my shirt fall to the ground, I look her over, she's fucking beautiful, Lief nibbles her shoulder. "Crawl to him."

"Crawl?" She scoffs. "No."

I motion her forward again with a wicked smile. She starts to refuse, but Lief whispers something in her ear that makes her blush and moan at the same time. He teases her pussy with one finger before rubbing that same finger over her bottom lip.

Her tongue follows and when she moves, I can see the sheen of her wetness on her thighs. She slowly drops to her knees, furious gaze on me as she slinks across the floor, moving more like a jungle cat than a needy woman.

She narrows her eyes at me. "I'm not making a habit of this."

"Of crawling or fucking two men at once?" I ask.

She blushes and bites her lip. After all the dirty things she said while I was fucking her, this is what makes her blush? I slide my hand over her cheek and into her hair before kissing her. I lick across her tongue and feel her relax into the kiss. She nips my tongue playfully and I draw back.

"Better watch those teeth, sweetheart."

"Or what?" There's that challenge again.

Lief's hand swats across her bottom, at half the heft I was using and she glances back at him, finding him naked, hard, and eyeing her like she's a good meal. She lets out a shaking breath and meets my eyes.

"This is okay?" She asks.

I kiss her again. "Better than okay," I assure her.

"You're sure?" This time to Lief. "I haven't … this is new. I'm okay with it, but if there's an issue, I want to know now. Not because either of you is pouting."

I chuckle and see Lief's lips turn up as he gets on his knees behind her. He kisses along her spine and her eyes flutter. "I want you, Valerie."

"I know, I'm not asking if you want me, I'm-"

But he licks her pussy and she lets out a moan instead of finishing her sentence. I kiss her hungrily, squeezing and rubbing her tit in my hand. "It's that simple, sweetheart. We want you."

She nods, giving in as she kisses me again. As Lief gets adjusted, she slowly kisses and nips down my body until I bundle her dark hair up in my hands. "Take my cock, sweetheart. Show Lief what a good girl you can be."

She licks from base to tip, then swirls her tongue around the head, making me hiss. Once she wraps her lips around me, she grunts and I see her eyes roll back. Lief thrusts into her again and groans, low and hungry.

Valerie takes me deeper, faster, almost like she can make me fuck her throat again. But when I get close, she slows, eyes on me with a wicked glint there. Ooh, she thinks she can make me pay for edging her earlier?

I arch an eyebrow. "You're going to finish what you start. Only good girls get to come."

She lets out a ragged breath, then moans around my cock as Lief ups the pace. She whimpers and bounces between us as she keeps blowing me. I groan and watch her try to control herself despite the obvious pleasure she feels.

Lief kisses up her back, across her shoulders, and then purrs something against her skin that I can't hear. She moans and takes me so deep she gags.

I reach for her, ready to pull her off and make sure she's okay, but she keeps going, a new determination ruling her. My head falls back as my hips thrust up and into her hot mouth. "Fuck, sweetheart. Just like that."

She moans again and keeps sucking me, hard and fast, determined to make me come. Once I fill her mouth and she swallows, her eyes flick to Lief. "Now?"

He nods.

He talks to her in another language as he fucks her, and I see her blush spread over her chest. Lief hauls her up so she's riding reverse cowgirl and I can't stop myself from kissing her tits, sucking and licking her nipples, feeding her my fingers so she has something to fill her mouth.

She whimpers and curses before moans take over, then she comes apart. Lief pants and grits his teeth, but then he comes too, deep inside her. He groans and lays his cheek on the top of her head. "Now you get what I promised."

"Mm." She hums.

"What reward is she getting for behaving?" I ask, curious.

"Cuddling." He chuckles. "And taking care of me."

"A very good reward," She hums, eyes only half-open.

I get dressed and both Lief and I help Valerie do the same. She gets Lief's pants on, then buttons up his shirt, earning a soft kiss. I take her mouth in something hotter, hungrier, and rub myself against her. "Same time next week, Dr.?"

She giggles. "We'll dig deeper into that brain."

"Sure. That's the only way we'll be getting deep," I tease with a wink.

"Your father is expecting you. Call him," Lief reminds me. "Or I won't be the only one here."

That sobers me. I huff and walk out the back, on my phone. I assure my father, in Russian, that I'm fine. I needed more time with the therapist to fill out some paperwork under the fake name and to set up another appointment.

Not that it changes that he wants me home now.

I hang up when Valerie and Lief come out. Valerie looks at me, takes my chin in her hand so I have to look down at her, and searches my eyes for something. I almost look away. I feel like she can see too much, that she knows too much now.

She gets closer and pulls me down so she can press her forehead to mine. "You are a good man, Hunter. You don't need your father's approval and you don't have to be an obedient worker drone. Love isn't earned. It's given."

I swallow hard and kiss her softly. "Thank you, Valerie."

"I mean it. Don't let him bully you just because he's the parent. You're a capable adult. I know you are. You don't have a curfew and it's good and healthy to set boundaries. Take care of yourself." Her eyes flash wickedly. "Or I'll make a house call and show you exactly how to."

Fuck, that's laced with such dirty promise and so much danger, I think I'm hard already. But my heart is beating fast in my chest, threatening to burst for that damn compliment, that assurance, for her.

Pushing it down, I kiss her again. I nearly revealed too much in her office already. Because Valerie is the exact kind of woman I could fall in love with and now that I'm tempted to show her more than my confidence, I'm afraid I'm going to topple over myself trying to win her affection before I'm completely lost to her.

She kisses my cheek. "Text me later. A conversation, not just your dick … no matter how much I like it."

I groan and kiss her again before the three of us round the building and I head to my car. Lief shows Valerie his motorcycle and she lets him talk, but her eyes flick to me again just before I leave, letting me know I'm not forgotten, I'm not second best, I'm not just an option. I'm a choice.

One she's made, because she wants me and not the millionaire playboy I come off as.

I take a sobering breath and drive home once I see Lief wrap his arm around her. He'll take care of her. He'll keep her safe. And I have my brother to protect from our father who is going to be more and more paranoid until we get this fucking leak solved.

When I get home, my father is waiting for me, alone, with one light turned on and a cigar in his hand. I glare at the cigar. He likes to smoke, but he likes to use those for pain more. I hang my jacket and nod to him.

"Traffic, I assume?" My father says.

He's trapping me. I feel it.

"No," I answer seriously. "A long and needed discussion. I had to cool my head and switch back to work mode before coming home. Confront my weaknesses."

His eyes flick to mine and he nods. "Good. Now go deal with your brother's weaknesses. He has some hesitation to look deeper at Lief. No one is more likely to be a leak than one I trust entirely, with the worst of what we do."

"Whoever suggested that is clever," I say, knowing he'll miss my angle.

"Sven has proven himself truly loyal recently," Father says as if agreeing. "I look forward to our business being taken care of so I can hand it down to you, knowing you'll protect it and those involved."

I'm going to do plenty of protecting. Right after I take care of the dickhole who is framing Lief for insubordination. The sooner it's taken care of, the sooner I get to make my own time for Valerie.

VALERIE

*L*ief follows me home, but when I park, I eye his bike hungrily. I'd love to be on it with him, clinging to him as the rush of wind tangles my hair. He pulls me against him tightly and kisses my jaw and my neck.

"We'll get food before I leave and you can ride," He promises.

Of course, he knows what I want. Doesn't he always? Inside, I get to wash him down in the shower, fingers stroking over every thick muscle, kneading into his sinfully soft skin. I feed him kisses, and wash his hair, enjoying all of it.

Then I get the pleasure of drying him, head to toe. I sink to my knees when he's hard and wrap my lips around him. Lief groans and cups the back of my head in one firm, calloused hand, helping me blow him.

Even after the multiple rounds with Hunter, and having them both I want more. They're a drug that I'm already addicted to, not that I can tell any of them that without losing my ground. If they knew how deeply they've wormed into my heart and head, they'd never leave me alone.

So instead, I dig my nails into Lief's thighs and give him the best blowjob I can, licking and sucking just like I've learned. Lief's legs tremble. "So good, Valerie."

I hum in my throat and his eyes roll back before he fills my throat with come. I drag my tongue over his length before popping off his cock. He lifts me with one finger under my chin. "I thought taking care of me would mean nothing sexual."

"I couldn't resist," I admit, trying to catch my breath. "Want a drink?"

He nods and follows me to the kitchen. I down two glasses of water and Lief slowly drinks from his icy glass, eyes on me. Pulling him to bed, I position him until he's laying on my chest, using me like a teddy bear.

I run my fingers through his wet hair. "What do you like to do to unwind after a long day of work?"

"I don't work consistent hours," He murmurs. "I get breaks throughout, but I'm often called to work more."

"All three of you have issues setting boundaries." I shake my head. "But the question is still there. Video games? Reading? Collecting stamps?"

His chuckle rumbles through me as he kisses my collarbone. "I enjoy chess." His fingers carefully stroke my side, but I can feel his foot bouncing too. "Reading nonfiction, mainly about history. I play piano as well."

"Are you uncomfortable?"

His foot stops tapping as our eyes meet. "This is new to me."

"Being taken care of or staying after sex?" I challenge.

He considers that for a moment, icy eyes glazing. "Both."

I nod and rub his shoulders slowly, massaging the thick muscle there. "I appreciate you staying with me. It keeps me from feeling like …"

But I don't want to tell him that if they always left right after, I'd feel like an unpaid whore. I know that's not what I am. Not to them. Lief kisses my jaw softly. "I also go to the shooting range."

"You have a gun?"

"Yes." Another soft kiss on my neck. "I like knowing that I can defend myself and those I care about. I learned to shoot as a teenager and I enjoyed turning my frustration and anger into something productive. I can fight sufficiently."

"Which means incredibly well," I tease. "You minimize often."

"I'm realistic," He counters.

"Yeah, how do you think you are at sex?"

He chuckles. "Sufficient."

"Like I said, minimizing." I stroke his cheek. "You can play piano, speak multiple languages, know so many facts, and I bet you're lethal with any weapon."

He adjusts on top of me, face hovering over mine as he straddles me. "I have the ability to protect you from everything the world can throw at you, Valerie. You never have any reason to be afraid."

I swallow at the intensity in his eyes. He presses his lips to my forehead. "I promise, pet. You'll never have a reason to be afraid. I'll protect you. So will Chase and Hunter."

"Why would I be afraid?" I ask. "I'm pretty good at dealing with my own shit. Remember how I almost tased you?"

He kisses me softly, his tongue gently stroking over my bottom lip. I can feel his heartbeat even on his arms as I stroke him. My eyebrows knit together and I shake my head at him. "What's wrong, Lief?"

"I worry for you."

I pull him down, wrapping my legs around him and drawing silly designs on his back. "I've dealt with a lot. I promise I can handle more than it seems." I close my eyes for a long moment. "My parents … sucked. My mom was only half there and always let my father have control. It was like she was afraid to speak out against him. Even when he was giving me hell."

"Valerie, I'm sorry that..."

"He never hit me hard enough to leave a bruise the next day, but he never hid how much I failed him either. If I got Bs. If there were typos. If I said something out of line. If I talked too much or not enough. Everything depended on his mood." I stroke Lief's back. "When I got older, I tried to protect my mother from him. I learned how to get in his head and make him think even if he didn't want to. It was only hard when he was drinking. But I'd just pour a little more alcohol every time until he'd pass out. My mom would never run. Even when I had everything ready," And I can't stop talking.

He kisses the corner of my jaw. I shrug. "I stopped trying. I just told myself I would never be like her. I would never depend on a man for self-respect. I would never let a man control me so entirely. I would never pass along his genes, his anger, her weakness."

"You're a strong woman, Valerie. But you don't have to do everything," Lief whispers. "Otherwise, what can I offer you?"

"Company." I smile. "Your fun facts. Soft kisses, kinky sex. Good memories and tons of happiness."

Lief's cheeks flush red and he kisses me hard, licking deep into my mouth before he pulls me up and hugs me. I blink a few times, then bury my face in his throat. "I like who you are, not what you can give me."

"I like you too. I like your independence, the way your mind works, how we talk. I like how you make me feel and who you inspire me to become," He whispers.

I open my mouth to say something as if I can say anything to those warm words that are making my heart beat faster. But my stomach growls. Laughing, Lief pulls me out of bed. "Come with me, pet. We'll get food."

And we do. The motorcycle is amazing, wonderful, a pure adrenaline rush. Lief weaves through traffic, hits speeds that I know are illegal, but I also know he's in complete control, that he would never let anything hurt me.

After picking up food and checking his phone, he takes me home. He pulls the helmet off me and kisses me after smoothing my hair down. "Beautiful."

"Do you have to leave?"

"Soon." He motions to the bag I'm holding. "After sushi."

"Come on, Viking. You have two whole rolls to eat."

And that's what we do. We share more about ourselves, even though it almost looks like it pains him sometimes, and then he checks his phone as I stuff an entire roll in my mouth, and his lips turn down.

"I must go."

"Okay," I say around my food.

He chuckles and kisses my full cheek. "I'll see you again soon. Keep your taser on you and those smarts."

I nod, show him out, and kiss him again, tasting the lingering spice on his tongue. I want to cling to him, get all three of my men – because they are mine, I refuse to share them with any other girl – in one place.

Another night. Soon.

"Be good, pet."

"No making boys cry?" I tease.

"Just not us." He chuckles, kissing me one more time before he walks away, gorgeous, larger than life, and a little more human than the last time he left.

Leif and Hunter opening up to me after holding out on me is amazing. Chase in general has been amazing. I see three texts from him, saying he's thinking of me, he'd love to see me soon for an overnight visit, even offering the yacht and his friends.

They're overwhelming individually and willing to share me seems surreal. I have to pinch myself just to make sure this isn't some intense dream. And then I need to thank my bestie and her men for the suggestion of trying out a polyamorous relationship. I smile to myself.

And I pinch myself at the office the next day. My last day before a solid week off thanks to Spring break. After talking to Diana and my other patients, I wave goodbye to Leigh – the head of the office and walk to my car. I get in and drive home, park, and pull my phone out to call Sophie.

But before I can, I see a flash of light. Looking up, there's Lief, talking to a man. I smile, and start to get out of my car, but then I see the man turn, Lief grabs him, injects something into his neck, then jerks him into a car. I gape, my feet shaking on the asphalt.

"What the fuck," I whimper.

Lief glances around, then his eyes are on me. Another guy gets out of the car, someone slightly smaller than Lief, but no less intimidating. I run. I don't think twice. I'm not going to trust Lief to protect me. I'm not going to ask him to take someone on for me.

I fit myself into an alley, then dodge behind a dumpster, accepting that my tits are probably going to be flattened and that breathing will suck. It's not my first time hiding in a place I don't fit.

But the man that chases me down the alley isn't my dad. This man has a gun on his hip, a knife in his hand, and murder in his eyes. I cover my mouth with my hand, making sure that no breath escapes.

High-stakes hide and seek.

Lief comes around the corner, looking more like death than anyone has a right to, and barks something in Russian. It's unflinching, sure, angry. The other man argues, but Lief shakes his head. The other one gets in Lief's face, shoves him, and hisses at him.

No reaction. Lief's face doesn't change remotely. The guy turns back around, kicking trash bags, then he's talking to someone else. I nearly slip, kick a can slightly and Lief's eyes flick to me quickly. He puts his hand down, almost like he's telling me to stay and I see a can at his feet.

"Was me." He says in English.

I cringe further against the dumpster as my vision swims. What the fuck have I gotten myself into? Why the hell does Gunner know gangsters or mobsters or even straight-up murderers? Nope. Not the time for that question, Val, I remind myself.

Just stay quiet. Don't move. Don't give in to crying. Not until I'm safe. I slide a shaking hand into my pocket and put it on silent. A text from Hunter appears

HUNTER: Do not run. I'll come get you.

Fuck no. Hell no. Absolutely not.

I'd rather run back to Sophie and her men than let him get me.

Lief and the other man keep going, but I don't move. I can't move. I'm too busy reliving the moment, seeing the sharpness of the knife, of remembering that Lief said he's good with a gun.

Hunter obeys his father. He and Chase are in the family business. So is Lief …. A company they won't talk about. They skirt around, distract from. A company that involves murder. I dig my nails into my hand to keep from fainting.

They're in the fucking mafia.

CHASE

*H*unter storms into my office slams the door and kicks my trash can, sending it across the room as napkins and take-out boxes scatter. He shoves his fingers through his hair and curls his hands into fists. I arch an eyebrow.

"Dad yell at you?"

"Lief and Sven got sloppy," He hisses.

Okay, those words are new. An entirely new sentence. I turn in my chair and face my brother. "How sloppy?"

"Valerie saw. Sven tried to hunt her down. Said she has to die. He doesn't have a name. Lief made sure he didn't find her," Hunter hisses. "She should have been at work. She never leaves early," He says.

"Lief went back to get her after Sven took off and he can't find her."

That gets me to my feet. "What the fuck. If our asshole father finds her-"

"He won't put a fucking hand on her or I'll make sure I take my inheritance early." Hunter snarls, furious, deadly, and ready to strike. He's never talked about taking over unless he was making it clear he didn't want to. "I will take care of Sven, messily if I have to. I'll rip out his fucking tongue. Valerie isn't going to be a casualty."

His phone rings and he answers it on speaker.

Lief's voice comes over the phone. "Her car is gone. I don't know where she is. Have Chase-"

"On it." I sit back down and start running her cards. She went to an ATM and pulled out three hundred dollars. I hack into the police precinct – because they never have the right security – and find her car info. I run a search on it and can't find anything. If I can't find it, Sven can't. Right now.

"And?" Lief asks, breathless.

"She withdrew cash. No hits on her tag right now. No credit card or debit transactions that I can see," I report, gritting my teeth.

"Try her cell," He orders. "She's running."

Hunter is fuming. He paces across the room, but I see something else. He looks older, ten years older as he rubs over his jaw. His hair is a mess, his suit rumpled. He's fucking terrified.

"She's smart," I whisper, still looking up her number, trying to triangulate. Finally, I snort. "Fuck this."

I call her. She doesn't answer. I shake my head and try again. Then again. Voicemail over and over. I send her a text, begging to tell me she's safe. Begging her to tell me how I can help.

VALERIE: FUCK OFF!

Groaning, I sigh.

"She could be in her apartment and have parked somewhere else, Lief."

"She's not that stupid," He growls. Once Sven finishes the drop off, he's checking the entire building. He'll have her name by the time he's done. Find her. Now."

He hangs up and I scrub my hands over my face.

Hunter calls her. He leaves a gravelly message, "Sweetheart, I know you're scared. Let me protect you. Give me a call and I'll get you out of the state. Don't go to Sophie. They'll follow. Don't go to family. Trust me, please."

He hangs up and we agonize for an hour. Finally, I see her phone in use. She's at some dinky fucking motel. I nod to Hunter and he's gone. Shivers race down my spine and I quickly get rid of all my search history. I put the blocks back in place, disengage, clear my history, wipe the drive of the data, and stare at my phone.

Two knocks on my door and then Sven comes in. He arches an eyebrow at me. "Lief is the leak. He let a witness get away. I need his location."

But Hunter and I have already talked about this with Lief. We know we're being turned in circles and so is our father. And we know that Sven has something to do with it. I don't know why, but I know he's involved. I know shit is about to hit the fan.

"Lief reported it," I say.

Sven blinks. "What?"

"Where do you think Hunter is? On a fucking date? He's taking care of the girl that you let slip. Lief was the one doing the hit. You were supposed to be watching for witnesses and some little bitch escaped?" I shake my head. "Are you on something?"

"No!" He barks. "Lief-"

"Followed protocol. You left a loose end. Fix it before Hunter does." I growl. He sputters, but I hold my hand up as I stand. Sven may be tall, but Lief and I both have more than an inch on him. "Lief is out there trying to fix your issue and cover your ass. Hunter is out there to make sure the bitch doesn't open her fucking mouth. What are you doing other than pointing fingers?"

Sven backs down immediately, but I see the hateful gleam in his eyes. He rushes away and I get the idea to look at who ordered the hit. Tracking things in the computer is easy enough. I don't see a formal order like I normally see tagged for Lief. And Lief gives me access to his phone. Based on that, Sven barked the order.

So I break a rule and head downstairs. My father looks at the 'conference' room with confusion. "Did you order this?"

"No." He snorts. "Sven said he had a clue on who may be the link and said he needed to pull this person in."

"They look pretty tongue tied to me."

We both look at the dead body in the room. My father rubs his head. "Lief-"

"Didn't deliver. He reported the witness and kept going after her while Sven delivered this like a fucking house cat before throwing blame at Lief," I hiss. "The same Lief that you personally trained, that has never failed in a single mission he's been sent on alone, has never raised suspicion. So why would Sven say that you ordered something you hadn't."

My father takes a slow breath and his eyes narrow on me. "Say it straight, boy."

"Sven's the leak."

Dad grabs me and throws me against the wall. "You better be able to back that up son."

"He came into my office and tried to say that Lief failed the hit. That it was Lief who let the girl go. But why would Sven bring Lief if it wasn't Lief who was meant to grab?"

My father's hand shakes. "Where is your brother?"

"Fixing your fucking problem because you couldn't see it. He thought it was Sven yesterday. Lief has had his suspicion for nearly three days. What's your excuse for missing it when you're supposed to see everything?" I snarl.

"Get the fucking girl," He orders, releasing me. "Then we can deal with this."

"Another innocent life because of your fucking incompetence." I quote something he told me when I was twenty.

I feel his gaze on me, but I have more important things to deal with. Valerie needs to get where we can protect her. Sven may be less lethal than Lief, but that doesn't mean he won't take her out and deliver her dead body to my father instead of her, living, breathing, promising not to talk.

If he kills her, it'll be a race. Lief, Hunter, and I will fight over who gets Sven's blood. I get halfway to my office before my phone rings. I get a room number and head to the hotel. I go to the room, but I find the door ajar.

There are signs of a struggle. I see Valerie's I.D., I see her taser on the floor, a broken lamp, a TV that's been dragged down. No blood. I don't know if that's good or bad. Then I get to the bathroom. The mirror is broken and there's blood here, splattered on the sink and floor.

When I turn, Lief is there.

He stares at the blood and his jaw ticks as his foot bounces. "It's not Valerie's."

"How do you know?"

He nods to a piece of glass on the floor. "She used it as a weapon."

"How do you know!" I demand, turning on him.

I don't know when I got this fucking possessive. When I got this wrapped around her finger, but if she's hurt, I'm going to bring down the entire fucking organization. Lief takes my hand. "Think about her for one minute. We told her someone was after her. She checked in here under cash. She refused to make a phone call longer than four minutes."

"She's been on the run before," I whisper.

"That mirror," he nods to it, and then I see a bra with glass splinters in it. "She broke it to get a weapon."

"And Sven would fall for that?"

"He wouldn't expect it. He doesn't know her." Hunter says, joining. "There's blood on the back door. I'm grabbing the footage from the owner. He's taking the bribe."

"I know what car he's in," Lief murmurs. "Already have a tracker on it."

"Did he know?"

Lief rolls his eyes. "Distracted him with cocaine."

"Any reason he'd take her?" Hunter asks, wearing a familiar mask of calm. He definitely got that from our father.

"To cover his ass."

"Any reason he'd keep her alive?" I counter.

Lief takes a slow breath and puts his hair up. "To pin our asses to the wall. She won't give him answers though. We know her. Think of how she dealt with you, Hunter."

"That's what I'm worried about." He hisses. "We need to find her before Sven cuts her throat for her attitude alone."

But I shake my head. She's smarter than that. She'll feel him out. She got Hunter to spill about his life. Lief's opened up to her. She's a chameleon and she knows how to take advantage of the moment.

"She's smart," Lief murmurs. "She's got longer than most."

"Longer if she admits she's been with us. Let's not let it get there," Hunter growls. "Get the fucking signal. We're tracking that fucker down and cleaning house."

"Hunter," Lief tries.

"Do not fucking tell me no!" Hunter snarls. "I can't stop teenagers from swearing loyalty or getting into debt with my father. I'm not going to let Valerie – someone who we promised to protect – get even one night of hell when we can do something! Fix it. Now!"

Lief glowers at Hunter. "You're not the only one who cares about her."

"Then stop arguing and get me answers."

Hunter storms out and gets on the phone in Russian. I follow him to get the footage and see Sven dragging a bound and gagged Valerie to his car. I zoom in on her face. She's pissed. She doesn't look scared at all. She looks like she's biding her time to bite him.

At this rate, we're going to be lucky if she didn't force a car accident. I rub my forehead and take a shaky breath as Hunter nudges me. "Alive."

"I have a location."

"Please tell me it's not the side of a road with police all around them." I motion to her face.

"No. The docks. Shipping area. We need to move quickly. That zone means no survivors. It means no check-in. No interrogation," Lief insists.

"No witnesses." Hunter's lips turn up in a wicked smile. Then he nods to the screen. "We're coming for you, sweetheart."

I look at her face. Something tells me she's going to put Sven through hell. He's got an uphill battle, but we're going to bring her home. I nod to her through the screen. "Don't let up, baby. Give us time."

VALERIE

I take in the man in front of me. Short hair, dark blue eyes, taught muscle. He has a scar on his face. I got some of his blood drawn in the hotel room before he used a towel to choke me. He tied me up, dragged me out, got me into the car, and threw me in the back and after I spent half the ride kicking the back of his seat like an insolent child, he drugged me.

Still, I have my phone in my jeans, between my underwear and my skin, just so he wouldn't immediately grab it.

My hands are tied to the back of the chair. If I can distract him and move just right, I can get to 911. That's a number of buttons. If I can get my phone, I can open my contacts and just keep hitting the call button until something sticks.

Luckily, it's not the first time I've been gagged, and this dick has a lighter hand, because I fought. I push it out and watch as he paces. He mumbles to himself as I look around. A warehouse. I hear construction or something outside.

A boat horn echoes and I nod. Near the water. Probably a shipping yard. Lief would know how far the sound of a boat can travel. But Lief isn't an option. He's just as bad as this asshole. I'm sure of it. So are Hunter and Chase.

My three gods are in some kind of Russian mafia and I'm caught in the middle. I should have trusted myself earlier. I should have seen they were playboys with a lot of money – more money than a 'consulting' company could provide and dug deeper.

I could have avoided this.

"Who are you?" I ask.

The man turns, glares at my gag, and reaches for it. I bite him, hard, digging my teeth in until he hits me. I fall over, giving my hand enough room to get into my pants as he picks me back up. I hit the button and tap the screen, happy I put the brightness down.

"Look, I'm not going anywhere, that's pretty obvious."

"Stop talking!" He orders.

"Is it your first time?"

That gets his attention. He narrows his eyes at me. "You know nothing, fucking bitch. If you hadn't been there …"

"But now you're in trouble, right? I wasn't supposed to see you. I wasn't supposed to get away. Sounds like a lot of pressure," I say, trying to remember where the buttons are. God, I wish I had a Nokia. "Whoever's in charge must be lazy as hell if they're making you do all this."

"I'm in charge." He grabs my jaw so tightly I can already feel the bruise. "As far as you're concerned."

"Oh, I know I'm not getting out of this." I shrug.

He blinks, takes me in, and leans his head to the side. "But no fight?"

"Not really much point when we know how this is ending, right?" I shrug. "Would just make both our nights harder."

He keeps watching me, with no trace of trust.

"You know, I'm a psychologist. If you need to talk, all I can do is listen."

"I don't need any weaknesses addressed."

"It's not always weaknesses. It's stress I help with mostly. A lot of people feel more comfortable talking to me because legally I can't share anything that's said. Patient confidentiality is important."

"Stop talking."

I do, for a moment, but I feel my phone vibrating. It pauses, and vibrates again, like a ring. I just hope it means I'm actually calling someone. It stops and I nod. "My name's Valerie. I'm in grad school right now and really need to have my life decisions checked if I've ended up here."

He looks at me again, just watching. He's pale, nervous. He keeps fidgeting. I lean my head to the side. "Are you okay?"

"I told you to shut up! I don't need your help!"

"Okay." I nod. "Then can you tell me why we're here? I don't know you. I don't really know what happened. For all I know, you're some undercover cop that's just making sure I'm safe."

"You're not that stupid." He snorts. "You know you're not leaving here."

"My patients will be upset." I bite the inside of my cheek.

When he doesn't answer and turns his back to me, I take a slow breath. What else can I do? He's a man, a conflicted man. Coming on to him would be risky. Really risky. I've tried playing innocent – didn't work. What will establish some kind of trust, even the shallowest kind?

I tremble and sniff. I'm fucking terrified. I am. Maybe I should show it. Just give in and be a little authentic. I could ask for a favor.

"Sir?"

He turns.

He stares at my face for a long moment as tears swim over my eyes. "Can you record a message for my mom and get it to her somehow?"

He walks to me and grabs my hair. "Why would I?"

"I haven't talked to her in years." I sniff. "I want her to know I still love her, even after everything. That I'm leaving her my life insurance so she can leave my dad and finally start her own life."

"Why would she want to leave him?"

I blink at my tears. "He's a mean drunk. Hits her and she thinks she deserves it. I ran when I had the chance, but she ... she didn't. I cut them both off so he couldn't hurt me ... I should have gone back for her. Please, just find a way to let her know I love her. It's all I can ask for."

He lifts my chin as my lips tremble. I'm playing it up a little, but it's what he expects. I can tell. He gently wipes one of my tears. "That's why you became a counselor?"

"If I fixed enough people, I could fix her. Or I thought I could. I just want to protect her," I whimper. "You understand that right? That's why we're here."

He considers that. "I had a very good friend. We were never supposed to know each other. It was wrong. But his son ... his son isn't as strong as he needs to be. He needs help."

"Then he's lucky to have you." I whimper. "I wish my mom had someone like you. Then she'd be safe. She'd be happy."

I pretend to wipe my eyes on my shoulder, but I roll them instead. Stupid fucker. My phone buzzes again, a three-beat vibration that tells me it's a phone call. I hit the button and continue.

"You'd be able to do more than I ever could," I say.

"You shouldn't have been there. It was just the wrong timing." He shakes his head. "Doing this ... is not something I enjoy."

I nod. "We do terrible things for the ones we love."

"I couldn't tell my friend something, and perhaps, in your last moments, you can absolve me."

"I can try, but I'm not a priest," I whisper, then sniff. "I'll listen though. I'm very good at that. And we have plenty of time. No one knows where we are."

He nods. "My friend was ... not pleasant. Much like your father."

"Oh?"

"His wife and I grew up together. I loved her. The love didn't stop because of another man and I ... I do not know if her child is mine or if he belongs to my friend. He named him a horrible name." He snorts. "Stefan."

I nod but try to note that. Stefan, the name sounds familiar. Where do I recognize it?

"When my friend died, he begged me to protect his son, to show him how to survive in the world, but our world is not so kind. Italian and Russian, making a place for ourselves in this country ... not easy. Take work where found. Do a good job. Survive."

"Not the American dream this country sells," I confirm. "You've done well for yourself, though. I can tell. You're here."

"So who do I owe? The man who may be my son and knows only privilege or the man who gives me job? Gives me good life?"

"You owe yourself, sir," I whisper. "You know what's right and you know what you need. If you live in service of someone else forever, then you're no better than a dog, right? And you're not a dog. You're a person."

He thinks about that for a long while. Then shrugs then raises a gun at me. He cocks it and shakes his head. "Such an idealist. So American."

"It doesn't matter. It's true. You'll never be free if you live your life serving someone else, even if they pay you." I sniff. "That's why I had to leave my house. I didn't want to leave my mom. I wanted to be a good daughter, but there comes a time for you to define yourself. Who do you want to be?"

He considers it, lowering the gun. I continue. "You know who you want to be. If you didn't, you would have already killed me. You lowered the gun. So talk to me. What am I going to say? Huh? Who am I going to talk to when I'm stuck here? You already said I'm not leaving."

"I do not *want* to kill you, girl," He says simply. "Needs and wants are different. My choice – you go free. Perhaps I keep tabs, make sure you don't talk. But I do that, I die. The boy dies."

"Or I could speak in your defense. That you did what you were ordered to do. You got me! You kept me quiet!" I insist.

He shakes his head. "Doesn't work like that."

"Says who? Your master? If he's so weak that he can't fight his own battles, then why don't you just take his job? You're clearly capable."

He pauses, the gun wavering in his hand. That's right. Let me in. Think about it. I'm not just some bitch. I'm a person. I have to make myself useful.

"Or you can pretend to kill me. I'll dye my hair. Change my name. I'm very good at disappearing. But I'll keep helping you," I offer.

"Why?"

"Why not?" I ask. "You didn't hurt anyone. You were doing your job. You don't want to kill me. I don't want to get involved with the police. Why would they believe me anyway? I want to help people. People are messy."

He does something with the gun, adjusting something. I sit up straighter in the chair and he sighs. "If you run, I will shoot."

"No running." I agree, but I can already taste the salty air, feel the sun on my skin, feel the circulation coming back to my fingers. I've got this.

And I did it myself. Now I can disappear. I can get away from Lief, Hunter, and Chase. I can escape this bullshit and keep my life in check. It doesn't matter that I want to be around them. It doesn't matter that I still crave their touch. That I want to wrap myself up in them and never feel this vulnerable or scared again.

They only bring trouble and I can't be the kind of girl that runs blindly into the worst-case scenario just to chase men who ...

I sniff and hide my phone in my pants as he reaches for my bindings. All at once, the door opens. The man, who's name I still haven't gotten turns, reaches for his gun, then is on the ground after an ear splitting crack.

I fling myself over, trying to break the chair and manage to finish pulling one arm free, then the other. I run toward the back, only to have two arms wrap around me. I'm jerked against a hard body, smelling like old books, sweat, and ... Hunter.

He turns me and crushes me against him, his fingers in my hair. "You're alive."

A sob rips from my chest and I grab his shirt as I bury my face in his chest. My legs threaten to give out, but another hand cups my face and I see Lief over Hunter's shoulder. Then a kiss to my neck and Chase is behind me.

It's too much. Being taken. Having a gun pointed at me. Witnessing murder, and realizing exactly how fucked I am, even with the three men I thought I could love wrapped around me ...

A low ring echoes in my ear as everything goes black.

LIEF

$\mathcal{H}$unter pulls Valerie into his arms honeymoon style as she faints. He and Chase walk her to her car and that leaves me to take care of Sven. My hands shake for the first time in years as I do the necessary things to ensure he won't be recognized or found anytime soon. Once done, I get on my bike and see a text from Hunter.

They took her back to her place. I meet them there, walking through the door and finding Chase on the phone while Hunter gently strokes Valerie's face. The tremor in my hand returns. She's no pet. Sweet, often, but the bite she has ... more of a viper than any woman should.

Sitting on her other side, I look at her neck, noticing the red marks there, thick and frustrating, just like those around her wrists. One is worse than the other, bruised and open. But the blood on her shirt isn't hers. And her chest rises and falls with each breath.

"She's alive." Hunter sighs, pulling her hand up and against her cheek. "So fucking smart."

But our battle isn't over. She manipulated Sven, got him to put the safety on, had him willing to untie her and let her free. If she can talk him down from his drug-fueled edge, she can manipulate us just as easily.

I almost believe she's been doing it the whole time.

She got me to open up to her when I've always been careful to keep myself a mystery. Hunter is more devoted to her than I've ever seen. From Chase's tone, he's willing to go to war with his father to keep her safe.

Going to her bathroom, I pull out the first aid kit, find alcohol, and soak a cotton ball. Putting it under her nose, she comes back, a disgusted look turning her features before her gorgeous dark eyes open.

She glances at the three of us and jerks her hand from Hunter, crawling back on her bed until she realizes there's nowhere to go. Her eyes focus on me and I see her groping for something under the pillow.

"Your taser is in the bathroom," I say.

Her eyes widen and I can see the panic worming its way through her brain. "Get out. All of you. Now. Get out!"

"Valerie," Hunter hums, then he studies her white lips, pale face, and damp eyes. "Take a breath, sweetheart."

"You don't get to tell me what to do!" She raises her voice, then pats her back.

"I have your phone," Hunter says. "We need to talk about this."

"You need to leave." She shakes her head. "You lied to me! You …" Her gaze flicks back to me. "I should have seen it."

"You weren't supposed to see anything," I reply.

"Oh, because that makes it so much better, Lief?! You kidnapped someone. You chased me down with that man! How can I …" She shakes her head and rubs her hands over her face.

177

Chase jerks his head to the door and I nod once. I know I need to guard us and give us time. I gently pat Valerie's ankle, not making a fuss when she jerks away. "You are stronger than you think, little viper."

With that I walk to the door, glance out the peephole, open it, check the area, then draw the top lock. I text Mr. Volkov that we have everything handled, then turn my phone off as I see Hunter ease away from her too.

He paces at the foot of her bed. Chase takes the spot beside her.

"Valerie." His voice breaks as he says her name.

She pulls her knees up but looks over at him.

"This isn't an easy position for you. I know that. When Hunter stopped hiding things and my dad brought me into this shit, I didn't know what to do or how to think. I tried to find our mom, tried to run, tried to say I didn't want this life at all."

"I don't want this," She whispers.

"And that's reasonable. You were just taken and barely got away with your life. But this is not what it's like all the time. We promised to protect you, didn't we?"

She hesitates, eyes flicking between us again. I can practically see her planning her escape. I cross my arms and lean against the front door. We're multiple floors up and there's no fire escape for her to use.

Something I hated when I first came to her place because it would be easy to trap her, but now …

"We did, we were just slow on the draw. And I don't blame you for not trusting us to fix things. Not when we kept so much from you. But if you would have known, you would have been in even more trouble, babe."

178

"I'm not safe when I'm with any of you," She whispers. "And I'm furious and scared and I ... this isn't the life I want."

"It's the hand you've been dealt," Hunter replies, direct and unflinching. "You can run. Sure. That would mean giving up school, giving up your job, and leaving your friends. It would mean losing."

She throws a pillow at him. "It's not a fucking game."

"No, it's your fucking life." He hisses.

Chase holds up his hand. "Valerie, look at me please."

She does, even if it takes her two tries to hold his gaze. She swallows.

"If you don't want to see us again ..."

Hurt and fury roll in me at that idea.

"I will respect it. But don't make a decision about your future while you're afraid. Don't do it when you feel like your back is against the wall. How do you think we got roped into this? I wanted to be an ethical hacker or someone who makes video games and look at me now. Hunter wanted to be a Russian Literature professor. Lief ..."

"Travel the world," I answer.

She trembles and closes her eyes again, pressing her forehead to her knees. "I need to think. I can't just ... you three are dangerous and no matter how much I like you, no matter how much I like fucking you all, I can't – can't justify being some toy you pass around when you live this life. I won't be collateral damage."

Chase's brow furrows. "You're not a toy, babe."

She meets my eyes. Maybe she didn't tell the others about her home life. Maybe that was an in the moment thing, her trying to connect with me, to prove that she and I are more than just good in bed together.

I take a few steps toward her, moving slowly, trying to make myself small until I crouch down by her bed. I reach a hand out to her and she doesn't flinch, so I slowly stroke over her shin. "It's not the same as what you went through."

"It's worse. My father didn't kill anyone," She whimpers.

"I'm trying to put a stop to that," Hunter says, still not looking at her. "We're all trying to be better."

Nodding, I ask Chase and Hunter to leave the room for a moment. They glare at me. I know they want to be involved in this. I know they're determined to say and do whatever it takes to keep her as ours. But they will ignore reality for her and I won't.

Hunter curses and they go into the hallway. Valerie lets her legs go and I wrap my arms around her, hugging her to my chest. She squirms at first, hits me, cries, then just lays against my chest once the remaining fight is out of her.

I kiss the top of her head and rub down her back. "This changes things."

"What? Me watching you inject some guy with drugs and then seeing you and your buddy hunting me down? No. That's just foreplay, right?" She scoffs, the sarcasm branding me.

Closing my eyes, I breathe her in. Dust, sweat, and salt cling to her, but there's still Valerie. I squeeze her a little. "I meant what I said. I like you. I will protect you whether you choose to continue with us or not."

"That's not a simple choice."

I lift her chin and stroke across her face, lightening my touch over a bad bruise. If he wasn't already dead … no. That's the kind of thinking that has us in this mess. She leans into my touch and closes her eyes.

"If you all were just colossal assholes who expected me to be okay with this, it would be so much easier," She says. "But you didn't tell me and being with you puts me in so much danger."

But she doesn't tell me no when I stroke through her hair. She looks at my hand, my two recently dislocated and fixed fingers, then my face. "I'll be stupid if you three stay."

"How so?"

"There's too much in my head right now. I need to be alone. I can't ... I can't think when you're all here telling me things, talking my ears off, and trying to make this seem right."

"It's not right," I whisper, kissing her forehead. "But you're worth us breaking rules, worth trouble at home, worth waiting for."

"Then wait for me. Somewhere else," She scoffs.

"So you can run?"

Her jaw tightens and her mouth opens, then closes. "You just have all the answers, don't you? I'm just a scared little girl who should-"

That sassy tone, the fact she's biting back, that she's not crumbling or caving, it's so intrinsically Valerie that I can rest assured this isn't a dream. It's not some hope-fueled dissociation. I tangle my fingers in her hair and kiss her softly.

Her mouth doesn't move for a moment, but then her lips mold to mine for a moment. I let out a shaky exhale against her lips as I hug her tightly. "I was scared, little viper."

"You're too big and lethal to be scared," She argues.

"Terrified," I murmur in her ear. "Of losing you. Of being too late. Chase is right, you're not a toy."

"No, just convenient then?"

I snort. "Not even close."

The door opens and Hunter comes back in. "We have to go deal with Father."

"Guess our counseling session made a lot of progress," She grumbles. "Still not setting those boundaries, Hunter?"

"Not when it comes to keeping you safe. Chase is going to stay with you until we get back. We're going to make sure no one knows who you are and that you're taken care of."

"I haven't said I'm still yours," She hisses as I let her go.

"I don't care. Ours, or not, you deserve to live without looking over your fucking shoulder, Valerie. Stop being sassy for five seconds," Hunter orders.

"Or what, are you going to shut me up?" She uses actual air quotes.

Hunter smirks, tips her chin up, and kisses her.

"There are plenty of fun ways to do that. Be a good girl for me, just one more time, sweetheart."

She sucks her bottom lip.

Hunter and I leave, but I don't have the strength not to look back at her. I know she's terrified, but I also know she's still interested in us. That war will wage in her head forever if something doesn't change. And I'm not ready to give her up. Not close to ready.

"Stop stalling. We have to go deal with my father," Hunter growls. "Chase will make sure she's safe and then we'll have all the time we need to win her back."

"You hope."

Hunter missteps, but nods. "I hope. Either way, we're not close to done."

"Hunter," I warn.

"She knows too much to be left without our protection," He says over his shoulder. "We're keeping her close. All of us will make sure of it."

VALERIE

*C*hase gives me space which I appreciate because I can't process anything in my head. I end up getting a shower, but after scrubbing my skin raw to get the feel of my kidnapper off me and actually washing my mouth out with soap because I can't believe I let Lief and Hunter kiss me, I just sit in the tub with the water beating down on my head.

A part of me knows that these are the same men I've started falling for. Did they hide their mafia connections? Absolutely, but has anything really changed? I chew my bottom lip and bang my head against my knee.

Don't be stupid, Valerie.

I can't just give them another chance because they're great in bed. Can I? God, what is wrong with me?

Sure, Chase took me out on an amazing date, he listens when I talk, he shares, he's eager to have fun with me and show me the world in a way I've never seen. Lief started opening up to me, and told me more about him and I had already imagined building a blanket fort or something and challenging him to chess. And Hunter ... under all that

183

cocky attitude, he's so much more. I sigh. He challenges me, makes me consider things in different ways, pushes my buttons, and lets me push his.

I've never felt for anyone the way I do for the three of them and the last few weeks getting to know them, and talking to them, all of it has been amazing times ten. But I have a life, right? And I should be protecting it.

"Valerie?"

I jump slightly and knock my shampoo bottle over. "I'm fine."

"Did you slip?"

"No, I'm planning to rebel with shampoo bottles." I roll my eyes.

The door opens and I see Chase's silhouette on my shower curtain. He doesn't open it, but I hear his knees crack as he sits down. "Thinking in circles?"

"Something like that." I sigh. "How did you deal with this when you found out?"

"Not as well as you, I think. I actually fought Hunter. Told my dad he was nothing to me, had everything ready to leave the country … but I just … I couldn't."

"Why?"

"Hunter's been the one consistent thing in my life for as long as I can remember. He always made sure I ate, even if he didn't. Helped me with problems I had with friends, made sure to spare me from hell for as long as he could. I couldn't turn my back on him."

I rub my legs.

"You don't owe us anything, but I'm going to be honest, we're still going to be around each other. We've done everything we can to keep your name away from the organization, but …"

"But." I nod. "My butt has gotten me into plenty of trouble."

"I thought it was mine that you kept complimenting when you dragged me up to your hotel room." He chuckles.

I smile briefly, then rub my forehead.

"I know you want to think, but thinking in circles won't accomplish shit and you know that too. Hell, I'm not sure what you *don't* know at this point." He sighs.

"Tell me something real. Something to make this all okay. Something that will erase tonight from my memories."

"Impossible, baby doll." He says.

Just that nickname heats my skin as memories from the yacht cloud my head. How tender he was with me, even when we were fucking hard, round after round. There was always a gentle edge. Proof he didn't want to hurt me, would give me endless pleasure, but never pain.

Tears well up in my eyes again and I sniff. "Tell me something."

"I always wanted to be a superhero growing up. Like Batman. He didn't have powers, but he had money, and I knew we had that to some degree. I wanted to help people, to protect them. To save someone and know that they'd have a good life."

"Well of course, then the mafia is the first choice."

Chase chuckles. "Obviously."

I pull the curtain back a little. "What?"

Chase pushes my damp hair from my face. "Try a few more counseling sessions with Hunter and you'll find out plenty I'm sure." He takes my hand. "You don't owe us shit, Valerie. But I hope that you'll at least keep counseling. I hope you know we'll all come to save you, even if you can save yourself."

With that, he leaves me with my thoughts.

I groan. Why am I denying them again? Maybe we could just be friends with benefits? I meant what I said to the asshole who took me. I want to help people. And people are messy. Aren't they just a consequence of life? And if we were thrown together ... well I'm not saying I believe in the universe doing any kind of plotting, but maybe were meant to be around each other on some level?

It's too much to think about and my mind is already so fucking cluttered.

I stay in the shower until the water is cold, then I wrap up in a robe and lay down in bed. I know Chase is on my computer, and I don't really care. I just tell him not to delete anything and try to find a dreamless sleep.

But I dream about my men, about them coming to my rescue dressed up as different superheroes. Then it takes on an erotic twist. The "thank you" becomes more than a kiss. I pull at their suits, wanting to expose them, to touch them, to memorize their faces.

"Let her sleep," One says.

Which doesn't make any sense considering Hunter's cock is in my mouth and his brother is licking my pussy like he needs it to live while Lief watches, palming his cock and waiting for his turn to join in.

A more intense touch rocks through me and breaks the dream up slightly. I blink and my men are here, none of them naked, none of them superheroes in disguise, just here and mine. Hunter runs his fingers through my hair again.

"Go back to sleep, Valerie. You need it."

I shake my head. The idea in my head is stupid. It's just lingering lust from my dream. It's just the thrill of surviving hell and having these three men trying to protect me from their world. It's absolute horseshit and they won't see it like I do.

But my body aches for pleasure. And I know they can give it to me in spades. They can fulfill every desire, no matter how dirty. I lick across my bottom lip and motion Hunter forward.

He arches an eyebrow. "You need sleep, sweetheart. Please don't sass me."

"Then shut me up," I challenge.

I see the shiver tease his back and he leans forward before hesitating. "I don't take orders and you're not ready for anything right now."

"That's my choice, not yours," I counter. "I want you. All three of you. Now."

"Valerie." Hunter's tone sharpens. "You are going through a lot emotionally. I'm not taking advantage of that."

"It's not taking advantage if I'm offering." I tug at my robe, pulling the sash free.

Absolutely stupid, but I want them. Even if it's wrong and twisted and weird. They saved me and I can't get that out of my head. They could have left me. They could have saved me and left. They could have just dropped me at a hospital or something after the fact, but they stayed here to make sure I was more than alive.

I can deal with the repercussions tomorrow, but I can at least grab some pleasure from tonight. And I want it. I want them. Idiotic, ill-advised, borderline insane, I know it's true. I open my robe and look up at Hunter.

His face is the only one I can make out in the darkness. He groans as he looks me over and strokes up from my belly button, between my breasts, along my throat, and to my bottom lip. He gently traces the valley of my lips, his touch featherlight, my skin buzzes in anticipation and need for more.

I suck his thumb, holding his gaze as I do it. This is my choice, no matter what it says about me. I'm choosing him, Chase, and Lief right now. Fuck tomorrow. It doesn't mean a thing. Hunter groans and pulls his thumb back when I lick over the pad.

His mouth comes down on mine and he kisses me passionately, cupping the back of my head in his hand. He kisses me again and again, holding me close. Each one is supercharged with something more than we had the kiss before. Relief, passion, hope, all of it in each and every kiss. I massage his tongue with mine, then open to welcome him deeper.

Drawing back, he turns me to face Chase. Chase cups one of my breasts and feeds me his own string of pleased kisses. He's tender, sweet, every sweep of his tongue a question until he lets me take over and show him what I want.

He groans and palms my breast before focusing on my hard nipple. He circles it with his thumb and then pinches lightly. "Are you sure, baby doll?"

I kiss him again and nod as I thread my fingers in his hair. "Yes."

Two hands spread up my legs and a soft kiss warms my ankle. Looking down, I find Lief. I nod again like I need to tell them all yes, that I want this. And Lief doesn't need another confirmation. He won't fight me.

He moves further up, pressing his mouth to the inside of my knee and then my thigh.

"You want all of us?" Hunter confirms, drawing my gaze back to him as Chase keeps fondling my breast and sucks my other nipple, teasing me with flicks and swirls of his tongue.

"Please," I say softly. "Leave me with a good memory."

Hunter kisses me again, hungry and demanding, giving me everything and holding nothing back. I tug on his shirt and he frees himself of it as I start working on his pants. He catches my hands and kisses my palms before freeing his cock from his slacks. I eye his length hungrily.

I want him, them, everything.

Lief's hands guide my thighs over his shoulders and he licks over my slit. My hips rock against his mouth and Hunter groans, wrapping his hand around his cock and offering it to me. "One more time. Tell me yes one more time."

"Yes," I say obediently. Then remember the bare minimum of Russian I've heard in shows. *"Da."*

That breaks whatever restraint was lingering. He taps his cock against my lips and I open for him, welcoming him to slide across my tongue and into my mouth. I welcome every inch as I lick and suck. Hunter pants and rocks his hips deeper into my mouth, pulling back just before he hits the back of my throat.

Lief licks deeper, his tongue flattening over my clit as he devours me. Chase groans and I feel him steal one of my thighs, holding me open so Lief can lick deeper, and give me everything without compromise.

Hunter moans and I see his abs shake as I lick his favorite spot, right under the head. Our eyes meet and he nods. "Such a good girl. Once you come for Lief, Chase will fuck you."

I take him deeper in lieu of saying yes again.

I want all three of them, as much as they can give, right now. I don't want to think. I don't want to remember, I just want to feel every bit of ecstasy they can bring me like only they can.

Lief groans and his hand tightens on my thigh as I rock my body against his wicked tongue. Chase holds my hair back as I work on taking his brother deep. "We'll give you everything you want, baby. Everything possible."

HUNTER

*V*alerie moans around my cock, her eyes shutting just to peek up at me again from under her lashes. Her lips spread around me as her cheeks hollow out and I can't imagine a sexier sight. She whimpers and her eyes flick down to Lief.

I'm almost jealous that he's tasting her, getting to lick up her sweetness and make her legs shake like that. I'll get my turn again. I thrust into her mouth, wanting her attention on me when she's blowing me.

She pants and takes me again, blowing me faster, showing me everything she has to offer and more. Chase palms her breast before wrapping his mouth around her nipple hungrily. We could feast on her like this all night. Hell, I was happy just to kiss her again, to really kiss her.

Valerie jerks off me as her back arches and her leg tightens around Lief's neck. "Fuck."

"Are you close, sweetheart?" I ask.

She whimpers and nods, her body rolling in a way I'm sure matches Lief's tongue. Her head falls back and her back arches. Chase chuckles and licks up her throat. "Be loud so Lief knows just how much you like it.

Instead, she grabs a handful of his hair and grinds against his mouth while trying to hush her moans. I turn her head back to me and kiss her before she takes my cock again with renewed determination.

Watching her squirm and writhe between us is a new high. One I shouldn't enjoy nearly as much as I do. She presses her face to my hip, moaning and panting as she comes. Her body trembles and she keeps trying to squeeze her thighs together even though Chase holds one and Lief's head is in the way.

He licks one more time, sure and clear before kissing the inside of her thigh. "Delicious."

My mouth waters in anticipation.

Chase moves and Lief takes his spot, welcoming Valerie's demanding kisses. Once she's had her fill of him, she looks back to me. I lick along her bottom lip, eager to taste her mouth and pussy at the same time.

So sweet with the spice of her biting my bottom lip. I thrust into her mouth again as she groans.

"Fuck, baby." Chase groans. "So tight."

Lief lazily plays with her breast, then his hand strokes down her belly to tease her clit as Chase fucks her slowly. Heat builds in my belly. Valerie is too perfect. Her hazy eyes on me as she keeps blowing me, cheeks red, hair wild.

Her fingers dig into my ass and I happily thrust into her mouth, giving as much as I'm taking. Her eyes roll back and it does me in. Her mouth is too hot, too wet, and she's too damn sexy.

I groan as I come, my thighs shaking as I grab the headboard. "Fuck."

She swallows every drop, proving again how good she is, then licks across the head before drawing back to take a deep breath. I'm not done with her mouth. I kiss her again, hungry and demanding.

She whimpers and squirms, but doesn't pull away.

Moaning around my tongue, she digs her nails into my ass again. She's close. Good. I draw back and turn her chin to face Lief. "Blow him, sweetheart. Show him what that sassy mouth can do."

"Please, Lief?" She asks.

He kisses her softly as his hand speeds up. "In a moment."

"But. Oh. Oh!" She looks down at where Chase is pounding into her, determined and shaking as he goes hard. "Fuck, Chase."

"You feel so good, baby. I've missed you. I've missed this."

Her body bows and she grabs Chase's arm. "Please, don't stop."

I grin and kiss her temple, then the corner of her jaw, right by her ear. "Are you going to hold out on him, Valerie? He won't let himself come until you do."

She whimpers and wraps her legs around his hips. I swat her thigh lightly. "Tell him just what you need."

"Just like that!" She yells as he changes the angle. "Oh, fuck, Chase."

Lief licks over her nipple hungrily before biting softly. He bites again, just as Chase slams into her and the combination pushes her over the edge into another beautiful orgasm. This time, she's twice as loud.

Chase shivers, pauses, then slowly rocks into her again. She gasps and he lets out a ragged breath. "Fuck, baby doll. I feel how much you like that. Your pussy is so wet for me."

She hums in her throat and slowly her eyes open again. Lief drags his slacks off and she goes for his cock so hungrily, I'm almost worried for him. He strokes her hair back softly, gentler than I've ever seen him, and lets her have him however she wants.

And Valerie wants him hard and deep. She gags on his cock, but doesn't stop. She just adjusts the angle and keeps going. Chase lets out a soft curse, then fucks her again. I rub my own cock as I watch her take them both.

Chase jerks out and Valerie pops off Lief's cock to wrap her lips around Chase, swallowing when he comes for her. He pants and kisses her forehead. I trade spots with him, determined to be inside her now that I'm hard again.

Lief groans and nods. "Just like that, pet. No rush."

She hums in her throat and his hand tightens in her hair. I smile, then look her over. All flushed, dewed with sweat, and her perfect pussy, bare, pink, and dripping wet for us. I grab her thighs and put her ankles on one of my shoulders before slowly easing into her. The deep groan I get in response makes my muscles tense.

She's fucking perfect. More than I ever expected out of anyone. More than I'd ever hoped for.

I rock into her tight pussy again and see her take Lief almost all the way to his base. Chase holds her hair back from her face while whispering to her, too softly for me to hear what he's saying. I groan and lose a fraction more control.

Valerie's hips rock back against mine, reminding me that she knows just what we're doing, that she wants to give us all attention, that right now, at least for tonight, she's totally and completely ours.

And I'm determined to make the most of it. I fuck her hard and deep, making sure to hit the spots that make her moan and her back arch. As she gets closer, I can see Lief fighting himself. He's on the edge. She breaks for me, coming apart and Lief follows, holding the back of her head as her eyes flutter.

She swallows, her throat working hard and I can't hold out. Not when every thrust brings me into heaven, not when she finally says my name as I pound her into the mattress. I just let go, coming hard as I hold onto her thighs tightly.

"Fucking hell," I bite out.

She blinks at us sleepily, obviously exhausted, but then she smiles. "That's one way to help me forget."

I kiss her hip. We get her cleaned up before taking care of ourselves and then Lief gets a call. He lets out a string of curses before stroking Valerie's dark hair back from her face and kissing her softly.

"Sweet dreams, Valerie."

"Be good, Viking," She says, squeezing his hand.

He gets dressed and walks out. Chase is all curled up around her, one leg between hers, his head on her chest. She strokes through his hair. "Your hair is really soft, Chase."

"Thank you," He hums. "I'll tell you all my hair secrets."

She laughs softly and presses her face to his hair. "You know I'm not going to run."

"I *hope* you're not," He corrects.

His phone buzzes, but he tries to ignore it. The second time, Valerie lifts his chin and kisses him. "I know you have to work. It's okay."

Chase hesitates, kisses her again, then gives in when it buzzes again. In less than two minutes he's gone, leaving Valerie and me alone. Something that's only worked well about once. She pats the spot next to her and motions me forward.

I take it. She rolls against me and rubs down my chest. I play with her damp hair and she hums in her throat but doesn't say anything. Probably for the best. She's not the only one who has a lot on her mind.

I'd tried to warn her at the counseling session that our world was messy, was terrible, and could ruin her, but she hadn't understood. And I'd been glad because if she had, nothing would have happened between us.

But now she has all the information. And I know that she knows. I have to choose between family, the organization or continuing with her. My father would let me have her ... until he met her. He'd be worried she'd ruin me. That she'd ruin *us*. And he'll allow plenty as long as my brother and I are safe – even if that's not the same as comfortable. I never understood that kind of love under his hard exterior, but after Valerie was taken ... when she tried to get us to leave ... it made sense.

"Are you saying goodbye, Valerie? Is that what this is?"

"Hmm?" She lifts her head from my shoulder.

"Come on, Dr. Hot Stuff. You wanted us gone then you want to fuck us?" I brush her hair from her face so she can't hide behind it. "Be honest. I can *always* take it."

She shrugs. "I don't know. Logic says to put as much distance between me and you three as possible, but then the emotions make it messy. Because you guys are the same and Chase already said that I know probably too much to be on my own."

"He's right," I tell her. "So we'll be checking in, even if you're trying to shake us off."

"Pushy." She grumbles. "I can protect myself. I got him to let me go."

"Sven was weak in many ways," I consider. "I still don't understand why he ..."

"Loyalty is given not bought," Valerie says, adjusting so she's sitting up and my head is on her chest. She rubs down the back of my neck. "He had a crisis there. Torn between his *maybe* son and the man who gave him plenty. He was trying to have both."

"Not an option in our world." I sigh.

"That's a glowing review." She snorts.

I swat her thigh. "I warned you that I'd ruin you. I told you we'd destroy you. Our world is ... too much."

"Pretty on the outside," She says, quoting our session.

"You were really listening."

"I tend to," She agrees.

But I'm still waiting on a real answer. I want to know if this is her attempted goodbye. She presses her face to the top of my head. "People are messy, Hunter. We're problematic, but I like to think we're trying to be better every day."

"I am."

"I think we might need to put a pause on what we've been doing, all four of us I mean. Until we can get the other shit taken care of. I didn't want any regrets, anything to make me give in when I say that, so I guess it's a goodbye of sorts."

"Of sorts." I sit up. "Because we're going to keep checking on you and I'm still planning on going to counseling. Especially since I can speak with you more openly."

Valerie reaches out to me as I get out of bed and drag my pants on. She stands up. "Hunter."

"You need to think, like you said."

"I still want you guys around. I still want you in my life, but I'm not some little kid. I can protect myself and take care of myself." She takes a slow breath and tugs my shirt from my hands. I arch an eyebrow and put my hand out. She holds it behind her back. "Listen to me."

I motion for her to continue.

"I have things to figure out, but you three do too. Because I like *all* of you. That means more than sex to me. That means you all need to make sure it's doable. With your world, with each other, with me. I still want you three around."

"Greedy," I tease.

"Your fault." She pushes my shirt against my chest. "I'm going to be here and I know that you will be too. We're going to figure it out."

I kiss her, cupping the back of her neck. "I'm not accepting your good-bye. It's a 'see you later' instead. And if I know my brother and Lief at all, I can promise you that they want to figure it out with you too."

"I like that," She hums.

We've already fallen for her, but she's right we do have plenty to figure out. Mountains of things to sort through. And I can't wait to get started.

Need More

ALSO BY BARBI COX

Charmed by 3

Seduced by 3

Join my readers group

Secret Facebook Group

Get Claimed by Him Free!

Made in the USA
Middletown, DE
19 September 2022